AUTUMN AT THE COSY COTTAGE CAFE

A HEART-WARMING READ ABOUT LIFE, LOVE, MARRIAGE AND FRIENDSHIP

BY RACHEL GRIFFITHS

For my family,
you are my inspiration and my world.

AUTUMN AT THE COSY COTTAGE CAFÉ

By Rachel Griffiths

A heart-warming read about life, love, marriage and friendship

Motherhood has been one of the great blessings of Dawn Dix-Beaumont's life but with her children's growing independence, it's finally time for Dawn to return to teaching. However, Mother Nature has other ideas...

Rick Beaumont loves his family but he's busier than ever. With his high-flying career, two children and a third on the way, there's a lot to juggle.

Battling expectations, disappointments and a few surprises along the way, Dawn and Rick find their commitment to each other tested to the limit. The next steps they take will be the most important of their lives.

So when the pressure mounts and an important decision has to be made, will Dawn and Rick's marriage become stronger than ever, or will it be time to move in different directions?

Cover design by: Emma LJ Byrne

Copyright © by Rachel A. Griffiths

All rights reserved. This book or any portion thereof may not be reproduced or used in any manner whatsoever without the express written permission of the author, except for the use of brief quotations in a book review.

1

Dawn Dix-Beaumont dropped the Lego bricks into the large plastic bucket and leaned against the wall. The colour scheme of the playroom had been chosen to create a fun and lively space for their children, but right now, in the early October afternoon sunshine, it was giving her a headache. The yellow walls, the red and blue buckets for toys, the turquoise and purple beanbags, and the green shelves, all seemed to be growing larger as she stood there. Swaying.

Swaying?

She slid down the wall to the floor and pressed her head into her hands. It must be low blood pressure again. She'd suffered with it in both of her previous pregnancies and it had made her feel faint and lethargic. Only it hadn't come on quite so quickly before. This time, however, even though she was only thirty-three, it seemed that her body was not going to take pregnancy lightly.

Thank goodness it was Friday and Rick would be home for the weekend. Since finding out about the pregnancy, she'd tried to rest whenever she could, but it was difficult with two children and a house to run. As well as a rabbit and a guinea pig to take care of.

Shit!

She needed to clean the hutch out before it was time to pick the children up from school. She loved the animals probably more than Laura and James did. It had been Rick's father's idea to get the children pets. He'd said it would encourage them to be responsible and he'd insisted on choosing the rabbit and guinea pig and paying for them. In typical Paul Beaumont fashion, he'd turned up one day with the animals, a hutch, a garden run and all the necessary paraphernalia for looking after the pets.

Dawn had agreed with the concept of pets making the children more responsible, but her initial suspicion that Laura and James would soon tire of the day-to-day care of Wallace and Lulu had been correct, and now it was all down to her. But she didn't mind. She liked coaxing the rabbit and the guinea pig from their hutch, as it gave her a chance to cuddle them both before letting them loose in their run.

Of course, Laura and James did love Wallace and Lulu, although Laura was more interested in maintaining their social media profile than her younger brother was. She regularly took photographs of them on Dawn's mobile phone, which Dawn then helped her to post to the Instagram page that Paul had set up. *Wallace and Lulu's Adventures* was quite popular and received lots of likes, but Dawn also knew that it was a way for Paul to connect with his grandchildren. He was a busy man – even since his retirement – but the convenience of social media meant that he could check in with his grandchildren from the golf course, or the club at the docks where he kept his boat.

Dawn got up slowly, stood still for a moment to ensure that her head was clear, then went through the hallway to the kitchen. She picked up the shed keys and headed out through the back door and into the garden.

The sun was hot. Forecasters had predicted an Indian summer for England, but Dawn suspected that it would probably last a few days then they'd be plunged into Arctic conditions. The good old British weather never failed to keep people on their toes. Gone were the days where she used to pack her summer wardrobe away by September then her winter woollies by April. There was no point now; it was far more sensible to have a range of clothing to hand throughout the year.

She opened the shed and retrieved her box of hutch cleaning supplies, as well as a bag of straw, then carried them across the garden. Lulu, the two-year-old floppy-eared rabbit hopped to the front of the hutch.

"Hello, sweeting." Dawn knelt down and opened the front of the hutch then held out her hand. Lulu's nose twitched as Dawn smoothed her soft smoky-grey fur. "Do you want to stretch your legs?"

She lifted the rabbit carefully out then let her into the large square pen made of wood and wire netting. Lulu hopped about, clearly enjoying the freedom to nibble on the lush green grass of the lawn.

Dawn peered back into the hutch, but guinea pig Wallace had not made an appearance from the sleeping compartment, which wasn't like him. Wallace was quite a greedy little thing and usually greeted Dawn with excited wheeking, especially if she had a carrot for him.

She lifted the latch then gently opened the front of the sleeping compartment.

And there, curled up on the straw, was Wallace.

"Hey little man, don't you want to go for a run?"

He didn't move.

Dawn reached out and stroked his silky white fur carefully, expecting him to jump awake and to see his little nose and whiskers twitching as he greeted her. She gently touched his small brown paws, which made him look like he was wearing socks, then his matching brown ears. There was no response.

His tiny body was cold and stiff.

"Oh no!"

She covered her mouth with her hands as tears blurred her vision.

Poor little Wallace, just two years old like his companion Lulu, had died.

And Dawn had no idea how she was going to break the news to her children.

Or how she would break the news to their grandfather and Wallace's Instagram following.

∼

Dawn opened the door to The Cosy Cottage Café and closed it behind her, making sure that her tote bag was firmly hooked over her arm.

"Hello, Dawnie!" From behind the counter, her close friend Allie Jones, smiled warmly at her.

"Hi." Dawn gave a half-hearted wave then hurried over.

"What's wrong? Are you still feeling queasy, love? I'm sure I have another bottle of peppermint cordial here somewhere. Let me get you a glass."

Dawn shook her head. "No. No time. I have to pick the children up in an hour and something terrible has happened."

"What is it?" Allie took Dawn's hand and squeezed it. "Not the baby?"

"No. The baby's fine. At least I think it is. I mean…" She took a deep breath as a wave of nausea washed over her. "I'm feeling really bad, so I guess that's a sign that the pregnancy hormones are strong."

She instinctively cupped her rounded stomach. She was around seventeen weeks along now, and she felt huge. In fact, Dawn was certain that she hadn't been this size until she was about twenty-five weeks pregnant with her first two. It was getting harder and harder to hide her bump.

"So why are you… upset?" Allie peered at her. "Looks like you need a drink. Sit down and I'll get you one."

"Oh, okay then. Just a quick one. Something cold would be lovely, thanks."

Dawn took a seat on the squishy couch in the corner by the front window and placed her bag on the seat next to her. As she sank into the soft leather, she sighed. If only she could just put her feet up and have a nap. Although it was cool inside the café, the afternoon was hot outside, and her t-shirt was clinging to her back following her short walk to the café.

Allie brought her a glass of bright green liquid.

"Peppermint cordial?"

Allie nodded. "Drink it. You look like you need it."

Dawn nodded and accepted the tall glass. Ice cubes clinked against the side as she raised it to her lips and took a sip.

"That's so good, thank you."

"You're welcome. Now are you going to tell me what's worrying you?" Allie took a seat on the sofa.

Dawn placed her glass on the coffee table in front of them and watched as a bead of condensation trickled down the side.

"I don't know what to do, Allie."

"About what? Is it Rick? Are you two doing okay now?"

Dawn met Allie's bright blue eyes and a lump lodged in her throat. She shook her head.

"No, it's not about us."

Although, if she had the time to talk about it, she would tell Allie that, yes, there were some problems with Rick. Things had improved slightly for a while but over the past week – possibly even longer – for some reason, they seemed to have deteriorated again. But perhaps it was just her. She was, after all, pregnant and exhausted, and it was possible that her imagination was finding issues where in fact there were none.

Perhaps...

"Not really. Things are fine with Rick. I mean... well... they're..." She bit her lip. She didn't have time to air her marital woes right now. "There's something more pressing to deal with." She patted her black tote bag with the white writing *#babyonboard*. Her sister, Camilla, had bought it for her when she'd been pregnant with Laura and Dawn had kept it ever since, using it as a makeshift handbag when the lining of her old one was too sticky with old sweet wrappers and snotty tissues from the children. Rick had bought her new bags for birthdays and Christmases, but they were always designer labels and far too nice to fill with dummies, nappies, wet wipes and all the bits and bobs she'd acquired over the years as a mum of two.

Allie nodded. "And..." She raised her eyebrows.

Dawn opened the bag and stuck her hand inside. She pulled out a small parcel and laid it on her lap.

"You've brought me a gift?" Allie smiled.

"Not exactly."

"Then what is it?"

Dawn passed the parcel to her friend. Allie touched the

pink tissue paper then peeled away the Sellotape that held the wrapping together.

"Oh my god! What on earth is that?" Allie grimaced.

"It's Wallace."

"Wallace?"

"Our guinea pig. He's dead."

"I can see that. If he wasn't, I'd be asking you why you've turned him into a bizarre pass-the-parcel."

The door to the café opened and Allie quickly covered her lap with her apron.

"Good afternoon, ladies."

It was Chris, Allie's boyfriend. He came over to their table, pecked Allie on the lips, then sat down on the reclaimed wooden chair opposite them.

"Hi Dawn."

"Hi, Chris."

"You okay there, Allie?" he asked.

"What?" Allie frowned, so Chris gestured at her lap where her apron bulged over Wallace.

"Oh... no." Allie's cheeks flushed. "Dawn brought something to show me."

In spite of the current circumstances, Dawn had to admit that Allie looked really well. Successful author Chris Monroe had returned to the village of Heatherlea that summer for his mother's funeral and decided to stay. His main reason being because he was head-over-heels in love with café owner Allie Jones. Dawn was delighted to see her friend so happy. She'd known Allie for a long time but only become good friends with her in recent years after getting to know her in the café. Allie had been widowed six years ago when her husband was killed in a car accident. But she'd proved to be a strong, resilient woman and had used the life insurance money to set up The Cosy Cottage Café, which was now a very successful business in the pretty Surrey village.

"Something nice?" Chris asked.

"Oh no! Not at all."

Sweat prickled on Dawn's forehead.

"I see. Shall I leave you two alone for a bit?" Chris made to get up but Allie shook her head.

"No, Chris, it's okay. Dawn's guinea pig died and she brought it to show me. Dawn, you need to get it out of here. If anyone sees it... I mean him... I'll have health and safety inspectors all over me." Allie moved her apron then handed the parcel to Dawn.

"Yes, of course."

"How did he die?" Chris asked.

"I don't know." Dawn's lip wobbled.

Allie slid an arm around her and squeezed. "Come on, love, it'll be all right."

"But the children will be devastated. And my father-in-law will be too. I'm sure that Rick's parents already think I don't do a good enough job as a wife and mother and this will just be something else I've failed at."

"I'm sure that's not true, Dawn, especially not where Paul's concerned. Although I know Fenella can be... challenging at times."

Dawn nodded, thinking of how her mother-in-law made her feel.

"Is this the guinea pig with an Instagram page? As in *Wallace and Lulu's Adventures*?" Chris pulled a face.

"Shhhh!" Dawn and Allie shook their heads at him.

"Oh dear... and Allie's right; you can't have a dead animal in here." He glanced around at the customers enjoying their afternoon tea and cakes.

"I know. That's what I just said to her."

"What am I going to do?" Dawn stared at the bundle wrapped in pink tissue paper. "Poor Wallace."

"I have an idea," Allie said as she stood up and beckoned to Chris. "Put him back in your bag for now and let's see what we can do."

Dawn slipped Wallace gently into her tote, then leaned back on the sofa and closed her eyes. She was so, so tired. If she could just have a short nap, then she was sure she'd feel better and everything would fall into place.

Then she'd know what she needed to do...

"Dawn?"

She floated through the warm water, weightless and completely relaxed. It was so nice to be light and free and...

"Dawn, wake up!"

"What?" She shot up through the water to the surface where bubbles popped.

"Dawn, it's three o'clock. Don't you need to get the children from school?"

Allie was leaning over her, with a hand on her arm, and Dawn realised where she was: on the sofa, in the café. She must have fallen asleep.

She rubbed her eyes. "How long was I out?"

"About forty minutes."

"Wow! Sorry."

"Don't worry about it. Do you want me to go and pick Laura and James up?"

"Oh... they won't let you."

"Why not?"

"They've really clamped down on who's allowed to collect the children and I had to list two authorised people, so I could only include me and Rick. My Mum couldn't even be on the list unless I add her as an alternative, and for that I needed to ask special permission from the head teacher."

"Things have really changed since Mandy and Jordan were at school." Allie frowned. "But it's probably a good thing. Shall I come with you, though?"

"No, you have the café to run, and it's Friday, so you'll probably have a teatime rush."

"Chris will help out."

"Where's Jordan today?"

"He's gone to London to spend the weekend with Mandy. She got them theatre tickets and a dinner reservation at a swanky restaurant. Max has gone too."

"How lovely." It would be really nice to get away for the weekend, to enjoy a show and a meal that wasn't interrupted by a child refusing to eat their vegetables or by the other one needing a poo.

"Well as long as you're sure you'll be okay. Anyway, I think I've sorted something out regarding... Wallace."

"Oh!" It all came flooding back then. Poor Wallace. She reached out for her bag and realised it wasn't on the sofa next to her, so she leaned over and spotted it under the coffee table. She pulled it towards her then reached inside but couldn't find the small parcel.

"He's gone!"

"What?" Allie's eyes widened. "How can he be gone?"

Dawn emptied the bag over the seat next to her: tissues, Tampax – that she currently had no need of – two lip balms, half a biscuit, her purse and an old dummy covered in fluff. But no parcel wrapped in pink tissue paper. No Wallace...

She peered under the table again.

But there was no sign of him.

"What am I going to do?"

Dawn watched as Allie tucked her blonde hair behind her ears and looked around the café. There were two customers sitting at the table by the log burner – they hadn't been there when Dawn had arrived – and the table by the other window was now empty, so the elderly women who'd been there earlier had obviously left. But they wouldn't have taken Wallace. Why would they?

"Oh no!" Allie smacked her forehead.

"Oh no?"

"I bet this has something to do with Luna."

"But she moved to Chris's with you, didn't she?" Allie had moved in with her boyfriend recently, taking her two cats Luna and Ebony with her.

"Yes... but she keeps finding her way back here. You know I don't let the cats into the café but Luna has followed Chris back a few times and she did sneak in earlier when the door was open. What if she—"

"Luna has stolen Wallace?" Dawn's heart pounded against her ribs. "What will she do with him?"

Allie grimaced. "She has a strong prey drive. She even toyed with a dead frog that she found on the road once. It was completely flat. I wrestled it off her and threw it over the back fence, a bit like a Frisbee, but she went and found it. *Four times.* So in the end I stuffed it in the bin."

"But this is Wallace!"

"I know. I'm so sorry. However, Chris has popped out to see a man about a guinea pig, so you go and pick the children up and I'll meet you back at yours. And don't say a word about Wallace passing away to Laura and James. As far as they know, he's still alive and well."

Dawn nodded. "Thank you."

"Don't be daft. What're friends for?"

She put her belongings back in her bag, even the fluff

covered dummy, then finished her drink and got up. Allie was right; she needed to head over to the school. She hated being late for the children and rarely ever was. The thought of them waiting for her as others went home with their parents and grandparents was too much to bear.

But as she stepped out into the sunshine, her heart jumped, as a piece of pink tissue paper rolled past her on the café lawn like tumbleweed in the Wild West.

Taunting her.

Reminding her that tiny Wallace was missing.

And that the weekend she'd been looking forward to, was not going to work out quite the way she'd planned.

2

Dawn ushered the children towards home, glad that the school run was over until Monday. It was only a short walk to the village primary school but she was finding it tiring, especially in the heat. The heat that seemed incongruous when the remaining leaves still clinging to the trees were the rich reds, golds and browns of autumn.

"Mummy, can I have an ice cream, please?" Laura's big smile revealed her pearly white teeth.

"I'm sure we can find something in the freezer," Dawn replied, mentally scanning her last shop to check if she had bought some ice creams.

"Me too?" James asked. "Please?"

"Of course."

Right now, Dawn felt so guilty she probably would have consented to two ice creams apiece. Anything to divert them from discovering Wallace's demise.

As they turned onto the driveway, she was relieved to see Allie waiting by the front door.

"Auntie Allie!" Laura flew at her, wrapping her arms around her middle.

"Hello, Laura. Had a good day?"

"Yes! I wrote a story and I'm going to read it on a YouTube channel and make lots and lots of money."

"I see..." Allie raised her eyebrows and Dawn discretely shook her head.

"It's all about Lulu and Wallace and their adventures at the zoo and I'm going to post photos on Instagram to encourage people to view it."

"Lovely. Well I'd really like it if you'd read it to me in person too."

"Yes, come and have ice cream and I will read it to you right now." Laura tugged at Allie's hand.

"Hold on!" Dawn unlocked the door then stood back. "You two need to get changed out of your uniforms. Make sure you put them in the washing basket and put on the shorts and t-shirts that I've laid out on your beds."

Laura nodded.

"Laura, no fancy dress this afternoon. It's too hot."

"But Mummy..."

Dawn shook her head.

"Oh all right then. Come on, James."

Laura took James by the hand and led him into the house.

"Did you manage to find a... uh... a replacement?" Dawn asked Allie.

"I did. Well, Chris did. I hid it round the side behind the recycling bins so the children wouldn't see it."

"Brilliant. If we can just get it out to the back garden then they might never have to know." Her stomach rolled. "I hate to deceive them but they love those animals and I just don't think I can face seeing them upset right now."

"Of course not."

Five minutes later, Dawn and Allie were standing in the back garden gazing at the rabbit run.

"He looks right at home." Allie smiled. "They'll never guess."

"I hope not. Come on, I'll get you a drink."

Dawn didn't like to say anything, after Allie and Chris had gone to so much trouble to help, but although the guinea pig was white with brown paws, ears and nose, it was about twice the size of Wallace. Perhaps the children wouldn't notice, and if they did, she could say that he'd put on weight. Although there was something else about him that was different too, but she couldn't quite put her finger on it.

Back inside, she opened the freezer and located two ice creams then she handed them to Laura and James when they entered the kitchen, thankfully wearing the clothes she'd put out for them.

"Thank you!" they chorused.

"Why don't you go and eat your ice creams in the garden?" Dawn asked.

They ran outside so Dawn stood still and listened, wondering if they'd spot the difference in their guinea pig. There were no immediate cries of shock or horror, so she released the breath she'd been holding.

"Shall we sit out in the shade?"

She poured two glasses of lemonade.

"Yes, lovely. I can't stay long though as Chris is covering for me."

"Oh, I'm sorry, Allie, I wasn't thinking. You head back now, go on."

Allie shook her head. "He'll be fine for half an hour. I'll keep you company for a bit."

"Thank you."

They sat on the wooden chairs on the decking just outside the French doors, and watched as Laura and James giggled together as they ate, sitting side by side on the root bench that Dawn had bought Rick for his last birthday. She'd looked online for weeks to find the perfect one. He'd hinted enough times when they'd visited garden centres and she'd finally found one that she thought he'd like. Her heart clenched. They'd been happy then hadn't they? And that was only in the spring. Before they'd got pregnant again. Before Dawn's hopes of returning to teaching had been replaced with thoughts of impending motherhood and how she'd manage with three children instead of two. Before Wallace had departed...

"Mummy!"

Laura was staring at the rabbit run.

Dawn pulled a face at Allie.

"Yes, love."

"What's happened to Wallace?"

"Uh... why?"

"He's HUGE."

"Is he?"

Dawn turned to Allie again and her friend pretended to stuff food into her mouth then waddled from side to side.

"Yes, Mummy, he's so fat." James was next to his sister now, peering at their pet.

"Well... he has been eating a lot recently."

"But he wasn't that big yesterday."

Laura turned her intelligent gaze on her mother and a small frown furrowed her brow, then she put her hands on her hips. Dawn had to fight the urge to tell her not to get sticky hands on her clean clothes.

"No?" She asked her daughter.

"Perhaps he grew overnight." Allie shrugged, as if guinea pigs doubled in size all the time.

"Hmmm." Laura tapped a finger on her chin and Dawn held her breath. Her daughter was very bright and it was something that usually made Dawn's heart swell with pride, but right now, she'd have been delighted if Laura had just accepted what she was told as the truth. "Perhaps."

Dawn glanced at Allie who winked in return.

For now, it seemed that Wallace's replacement had been accepted, although for how long, she had no idea.

And she couldn't help wondering, and worrying, about what had happened to Wallace the first.

Dawn kissed James's forehead then padded out of his room, making sure that she left the door ajar. She went into Laura's room and found her daughter staring out of the window that overlooked the back garden.

"Laura? What's wrong?"

"I'm just checking that Wallace and Lulu are okay."

"Of course they are. We tucked them in after you had dinner."

Laura shook her head. "Lulu won't have much room now because Wallace is so fat."

"They'll be fine, angel. Don't worry now."

Laura allowed herself to be led to her bed.

"Why didn't you want to listen to the story with James tonight?"

Laura shrugged.

"I thought you liked the Big Book of Fairy-Tales."

"I like it when Daddy reads to us."

"I know you do and I like that too."

Since the summer, Rick had made the effort to be home in time most nights to read to the children. But more recently, he seemed to be getting later and later each night.

"When will he be home?"

Dawn smoothed her daughter's soft hair back from her face. Her heart ached for her children when they missed Rick.

"He sent me a text to say he'll be back soon."

"When is soon?"

Dawn sighed. "In about an hour. The trains were delayed."

"Again?" Laura scowled. "I hate the train men."

"Do you want to read your story to me again?" Dawn asked, hoping to distract her daughter.

"No, I want to go to sleep now."

"Okay then. Goodnight sweetheart."

She tucked the covers around Laura then got up and crossed the room, switching off the light at the doorway.

"Night Mummy. I love you."

"I love you too."

Dawn turned away, the lump in her throat threatening to choke her. Damn Rick and his delayed trains. No, damn the delayed trains. It wasn't Rick's fault, she was sure of it. He was trying to provide for his family and she knew he couldn't rush out of the office before his colleagues. The world of investment banking that he worked in was a tough one and she knew that competition amongst employees was fierce.

But she did wish that he could try a bit harder to get home before nine, at least a few times a week. Surely that wouldn't be too much to ask?

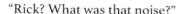

"Rick? What was that noise?"

Dawn reached out to pat her husband but his side of the bed was empty.

"Rick?"

Her heart raced as she tried to fight the sleep fog.

There it was again. A clinking sound coming from downstairs. She'd have to go and investigate, as it seemed that she was alone with the children. Rick hadn't come home by ten and she was exhausted, so she'd gone up to bed, telling herself she'd read until he returned but she must have fallen asleep as soon as she lay down.

She pulled her dressing gown over her pyjamas then scanned the room, hoping to find a weapon. The only thing she could see was a coat hanger dangling over the door handle, so she grabbed it.

"Ready or not... death by Debenhams size 12-14 hanger."

She padded down the stairs, her bare feet sinking into the plush fibres of the carpet, and made her way across the hallway and through to the kitchen and the source of the noise.

She raised the coat hanger above her head and took a deep breath, ready to scream if need be, then launched herself into the kitchen.

"Who the hell do you think you are?" she screeched, as she spotted the intruder in front of the fridge with the door open and his back to her.

"Wha..." He turned around and as he did, she realised that it was Rick.

"Shit, Rick, you scared the hell out of me."

Her heart thudded and nausea flooded through her,

filling her mouth with saliva and bringing her hand automatically to her mouth.

"Who were you expecting?"

She lowered her hand slowly. "I thought we'd had a break-in."

He shook his head. "Don't be daft. In this neighbourhood?"

In the blue light from the fridge, his lean physique was shown to advantage in his expensive shirt and suit trousers. His jacket had been slung onto the kitchen island, as if he'd been in a rush to get something to eat.

"It could happen," she replied, feeling foolish at her sleep-fuddled reaction, then turned the light on.

"Hopefully not."

He closed the fridge then opened his arms.

"Anyway, how's my beautiful wife?"

"Tired. Sleepy. Recovering from the fright of thinking we had an intruder."

"Got a hug for me?"

She nodded then walked into his embrace.

As he wrapped his arms around her, she sighed against his chest. She loved him so much but sometimes he irritated the hell out of her. Yes, she was pregnant and her hormones were all over the place, but that didn't mean that she was an idiot. Not that Rick was suggesting that she was, but she felt that way when he came over all cool-headed and in control.

"Sorry I'm late. Between trying to get out of the office and the train being delayed again, I thought I'd never get home."

"The children missed you."

"It's the weekend now, though. I'll make it up to you all."

He squeezed her tight.

"Are you hungry?"

"Starving."

"There's lasagne in the fridge."

"You are the best wife, you know that?"

She slipped out of his arms and set about warming him some food.

When she placed his dinner and a large glass of red wine on the oak dining table in front of him, he caught her hand and kissed it.

"Sit with me?"

"I would, Rick, but I'm exhausted. I need to go back to bed."

"Okay, well I'll eat this then follow you up."

She nodded.

"See you in a bit."

She left the kitchen, her heart heavy and her stomach churning, because something just wasn't adding up. Her husband had hugged her and seemed to be loving as ever, but she knew that years of competing in a high-pressured work environment had enabled him to perfect a cool, collected demeanour, even if inside his blood pressure was sky-high. Something about the way he'd felt when he held her close was off: he was too thin now, his body leaner than it used to be, as if the slight softening that had come with contentment and being a father had been eroded away. But by what? He had been working hard, putting in long hours, and when he was home, he was always doing something around the house or garden. So it was probably just that and her own insecurities rooted in her self-consciousness about her changing body, as it once again became rounder and softer.

She was probably finding problems where there were none.

But as she climbed the stairs, she heard a familiar

sound; it was Rick's mobile letting him know that he'd received a text message.

And she couldn't help wondering who would be texting her husband so late at night.

3

As Dawn strolled along in the Saturday morning sunshine, she breathed deeply of the October air. Laura and James were just ahead of her, and her husband was at her side, her hand clasped in his. Everything seemed perfect. And that was the problem, the fact that to an outsider, they would appear to be the perfect little family, but Dawn knew differently.

Rick had not come to bed until gone two. What he'd been doing until then, she had no idea. She'd lain in bed, hoping that he'd come and cuddle her, spoon her in the way she found so comforting and that helped her drop off to sleep when she was at her most insecure. When he hadn't come, she'd strained to listen, to see if he was perhaps watching TV or loading his plate and glass into the dishwasher. She'd heard nothing. Then she'd fallen asleep, only to wake when he climbed into bed next to her and rolled onto his side, facing away.

She had sensed his tension, known that even though the hour was late, he had stared at the window until she'd drifted off again, a deep sadness tugging at her heart and fear gnawing at her edges.

When she'd risen at six, she'd rushed to the family bathroom where she'd dry retched over the toilet, not wanting to use the ensuite in case she disturbed Rick. James had come to the door and she'd had to pull herself together then, to reassure him that she was fine and just had a tummy bug. They hadn't yet told the children about the baby; they'd been waiting for the twenty-week scan to ensure that everything was all right and to give themselves some time to prepare mentally and emotionally, but as she was getting so big, she didn't think they could wait that long.

Perhaps today was the day...

"Penny for them." Rick squeezed her hand.

"I was just thinking about the baby and when we should... you know." She nodded at the children.

"I guess we can't keep it a secret forever. We could do it over breakfast? Or lunch tomorrow at your Mum's?"

She tried to work out his tone. Was it light-hearted and positive or was it forced, hiding something that he was struggling with.

"Really?" She glanced at him and her heart fluttered. She still found him so handsome. Even though they'd been together since university and had two children, he was still, in her eyes, the most attractive man she'd ever seen.

"Why not?"

"Thank you for this... taking us to the café for breakfast. It was a good idea."

"I like to spoil my family but I don't get the chance that often." He laughed but it sounded hollow, even outside on such a beautiful morning.

They reached the front gate of The Cosy Cottage Café and Rick opened it then stood back to let them all in first.

Dawn's spirits rose; she loved coming to the café. It was such a warm and welcoming place to be and she felt safe there. Allie was a dear friend and they'd enjoyed many mornings with coffee and cake as well as some uplifting Tuesday evenings, when Allie, Dawn, her sister, Camilla, and their friend Honey, would gather together and eat, drink and put the world to rights. On those occasions they often laughed until tears ran down their faces and it felt so good to have such close friends, so good to be alive.

The café garden was breathtakingly beautiful in the sunlight. In the borders, orange, red and yellow hardy chrysanthemums bloomed in the mild October climate. Purple-blue spikes of lavender still towered above silver-grey foliage, its sweet crisp scent permeating the morning air. Creamy white dahlias swayed in the gentle breeze, their centres of their multi-layered heads a soft baby pink.

Suddenly, tears pricked Dawn's eyes as she recalled something she'd once read about the flowers. Apparently, the Victorians had used the dahlia to signify a lasting bond between two people, a lifelong commitment. She had always thought that she would be with Rick forever, but recently, she was starting to wonder if he felt the same way.

She blinked hard and gazed instead at the café itself, a converted old stone cottage with ivy climbing its front, pretty purple shutters adorning the windows and a traditional thatched roof. On the side of the building, a sign in the shape of a teapot glinted in the sunshine and a specials board stood to the side of the front steps next to some colourful milk urn planters.

Laura and James stopped at the door and turned to their parents, so Dawn nodded at them to go inside. She was about to follow when Rick tugged at her hand.

"Are you okay, Dawn? You seem distant this morning."

I seem distant?

She swallowed the words, not wanting to cause a row when Rick was clearly trying.

"I'm fine. It's just... something happened yesterday and because you were so late home, I haven't had the chance to talk to you about it yet."

"What was it?" His hazel eyes roamed her face and she found herself leaning towards him as if hypnotised by the golden ring that flashed at their core, as if he had trapped the sunlight there and pierced it with the fathomless black of his pupils.

"Something happened to—"

"Mum! I need a poo!"

Dawn started. James stood in the doorway hopping from foot to foot.

"To what?" Rick frowned, clearly concerned by what she was about to divulge.

"Mum! Quickly..." The speed of James's hopping had increased and his little face was scrunched up as if he was in pain.

"Oh it doesn't matter. I can tell you later."

Rick nodded but as he released her hand, he whispered, "Surely he should be able to go to the toilet alone by now?"

Dawn bit her lip then walked inside. That was the problem with having an absent husband. He didn't understand what she dealt with on a daily basis, the type of things she didn't like to bother him with when he came home from work fit to drop. He didn't know that James had a phobia of public toilets – that had left the little boy nervous about getting locked in – following an incident in a toilet at school. Her own mother, Allie, and other mothers she knew had all tried to reassure her that children had their quirks and idiosyncrasies, and that, if not dramatized, such things would pass. But she still worried that James would be scarred by what had happened; he was such a sensitive boy.

How many things did she fail to share with Rick these days because he was tired or she was tired or because it just seemed like too much effort?

She waved at Allie, who was standing behind the counter, as she headed towards the café toilet where she would wait outside the door just in case James started to panic. It wasn't glamorous, it wasn't much fun, but it was motherhood, and Dawn wondered if Rick had any understanding at all of her world now, or if he just couldn't see past his own expectations and preconceptions of how things should be.

Half an hour later, Dawn was cutting up a cinnamon waffle for James. Laura was tucking into her lemon and blueberry muffin and Rick was working his way through a full cooked breakfast. Dawn had nibbled at a piece of toast but her appetite appeared to have stayed at home.

"Everything all right?" Allie asked as she filled the children's glasses with freshly squeezed orange juice.

"Delicious, thank you." Rick raised his mug of tea. "If I ate here every morning, I'd get fat."

"If you just slowed down a bit..." The comment slipped from Dawn's mouth and she sucked in a breath. But no one seemed to notice.

"Can I get you something else, Dawnie?" Allie placed a cool hand on her shoulder. "It doesn't look like that's tempting you. How about some yogurt and honey? Perhaps with a banana?"

"No, I'm okay, thanks. Just eating in the morning is difficult." She bit her lip and eyed her children but they didn't seem to pick up on her slip.

"I know." Allie nodded. "I'll be back in a minute."

She disappeared and Dawn was left with her family again.

"I like waffles, Mummy," James said. "Can we have them every day?"

"If we did, you'd soon get tired of them, darling."

Dawn thought of the different cereals she'd tried to tempt him, of the variety of scones and pancakes she'd baked that had soon been rejected, and of the mornings when she'd been on the brink of tears because her children just didn't want what she had to offer them for breakfast. Sometimes, parenting was so difficult; especially when you were doing it alone.

She shook herself. Why was she dwelling on negatives when she had her beautiful family right here with her and they were all enjoying their selections from Allie's gorgeous menu? She had so much to be grateful for.

Laura finished her muffin then drained her glass. "That was delicious, thank you." She got up and went round the table to Rick and hugged him.

"Hey what was that for?"

"I love you, Daddy. Are you staying home today?"

"Of course I am. It's Saturday."

Laura smiled then kissed his cheek. "You can help me play with Lulu and Wallace and take some new photos of them for Grandpa and Instagram. You should see how fat Wallace is."

"Really? Have you been overfeeding him?"

Laura shook her head.

"He's just put on some weight." Dawn winked when Rick met her eyes.

"Oh he has, has he? Well perhaps we better put him through guinea pig boot camp."

"What's a boot camp?" James asked as he dipped a piece of waffle into his juice.

"It's somewhere that people can go to exercise."

"Is that with soldiers?"

"How'd you know that, Laura?" Rick asked his daughter.

"Saw it on TV."

Rick grinned at Dawn and she shook her head. "Must have seen it at my Mum's."

Allie returned with a small plate.

"What's this?" Dawn asked as she met her friend's eyes.

"Ginger cookies. I baked them yesterday with stem ginger. They might help with the nausea."

"Thank you so much."

"No problem. I'll pack some up for you to take home, too."

Dawn picked up a cookie and sniffed it. The warming aroma of ginger made her mouth water and she took a bite. The cookie was fresh and crumbly with the gentle heat of the fragrant spice warming her mouth and tongue.

"Mmmm. It's delicious."

"I'm going to see Chris," James announced as he slid off his chair.

"James, Chris is busy. Don't bother him."

"It's okay," Allie said. "Chris won't mind. Come on, James."

She took his hand and led him over to her boyfriend.

"I'm going too." Laura jumped down and rushed over to the leather sofa by the window, where Chris was sitting with his laptop on his knees.

"Sorry you're still feeling queasy. It'll pass soon though, right?" Rick reached across the table to take Dawn's hand.

"I hope so. It's draining feeling like I'm going to throw up all the time and it had passed well before this point when I was carrying Laura and James. Sorry." She pointed at his plate.

"Don't worry. You won't put me off."

"Are we going to tell them about the baby tomorrow?"

"I think we should."

Dawn peered behind Rick to see Laura and James sitting either side of Chris as he showed them something on the screen of his laptop.

"I need to tell you something, too."

Rick nodded then placed his knife and fork on the empty plate.

"Go ahead."

"Yesterday, I went to clean the hutch out as usual. And I found—"

"A rat! A big fat white rat!" Judith Burnley, an elderly lady from the village, had entered the café and her words cut Dawn off.

"You don't say." Her companion, a woman of around seventy, shuddered as they approached the counter.

Dawn watched them, her mouth hanging open.

"Dawn, what is it?"

"Shhh."

"Don't shhh me."

She waved a hand at Rick then got up and went to the counter where she stood behind Mrs Burnley.

"Did you hear that, Allie?" Mrs Burnley asked.

"I did." Allie flashed a glance at Dawn. "You *saw* a rat?"

"Not exactly." The elderly woman drummed her nails on the counter. "Your cat, the grey one, dropped it on my doorstep then ran away."

"Oh. Do you mean Luna?"

"That's the one. Total nuisance that cat, always leaving dead rodents on my step. Have to scrub it with bleach on a daily basis."

"I am sorry, Mrs Burnley. But usually that's a sign that a cat likes you."

Mrs Burnley sniffed. "Only since you moved in with Chris."

Dawn processed the information. Mrs Burnley lived a few doors down from Chris Monroe and Allie, and it seemed that Allie's one cat, Luna, had been leaving gifts for Mrs Burnley.

But a fat white rat?

"It had no tail either. The cat must have eaten it first."

Dawn gasped and Mrs Burnley turned to look at her.

"I know. Disgusting, isn't it?"

Dawn nodded. "Uh... What did you do with the... rat?"

"Threw it in the bin, of course."

"The bin in your front garden?"

"Yes, of course." The older woman frowned at her.

"Right. Okay. Uh... thanks." Dawn turned and hurried back over to Rick.

"What was all that about?"

She took a shaky breath as a wave of nausea hit.

"Dawn?"

"I don't think it was a rat."

"What was it then?"

"I think it was Wallace."

"Wallace?" His eyebrows shot up his forehead. "You need to tell me what's been going on," he said.

And she did. Quickly, before the children returned to the table. She told him about finding Wallace and about him disappearing from her bag and about how she'd found the pink tissue paper outside and about Allie and Chris producing a replacement.

Rick listened carefully, then nodded. "So I'll go and check her bin. Make sure."

"Please. I don't know if I could face it."

"If it's him... I'll pop him home then come back for you."

He pecked her on the lips, then said something to the children, before leaving the café.

And Dawn sat there with her half-eaten ginger biscuit in her hand and her mug of tea going cold, wondering how she would cope if she ever lost him.

4

The next day, Dawn was peeling potatoes in her mother's small kitchen. Rick and the children were in the garden playing catch.

"They all seem happy," Jackie Dix said as she gazed out of the window at Rick and her grandchildren.

"They are. It's good for them to have some time together."

"Rick still working late?"

Dawn nodded. "He has a lot on, Mum."

"I understand that, love."

Her mother turned to her and Dawn met her green eyes, so much like her own and Camilla's, yet they carried something within them that told of hard times and disappointment.

"He's a good man, Mum."

"I know. But even so, good men can change if their heads get turned."

"Please don't."

Her mother shook her head. "I don't mean to, Dawn. It's just…"

"Not everyone is like Dad."

"Nope. You're right. I just get scared for you and Camilla... and for my grandchildren. I don't want to see any of you hurt."

Dawn bit her tongue. Her mother had a heart of gold but she'd never recovered after her husband's betrayal. He left when Dawn was eight and Camilla was ten, and now ran a bar in Benidorm with his third wife. Jackie had struggled to bring up her girls, working as a cleaner at several locations and taking in ironing just to make ends meet. Dawn admired her mother for what she'd done but also worried about her, as she'd never got over losing her husband. Although sometimes, it was almost as if she couldn't allow herself to move on.

"I won't be. Rick won't hurt me."

"I thought the same about your father a long time ago but I was blinded by love and lust. Fool that I was back then. I suspected that he was having an affair but I tried to ignore it. I loved our family life so much and the idea that he would risk it all for a fling was more than I could bear to entertain." She shook her head. "Then the worst happened. I sometimes think it would have been better if he'd just died. At least he wouldn't have chosen to leave us all then."

Dawn's mouth fell open.

"Oh, love, don't mind me. Forget I said that." She rubbed Dawn's arm. "Anyway, how're you feeling?"

"Not too bad this morning." Dawn was glad of the change of topic. "Allie gave me some ginger biscuits and some more of that peppermint cordial and the combination seems to be helping. Here," she handed her mother the colander of potatoes, "all done."

"Right, you go outside and play with your husband and children and I'll finish up here."

"Thanks, Mum."

Dawn hugged Jackie then went out into the small back garden, her heart heavy with the knowledge of her mother's pain.

"Another cracking roast, Jackie." Rick rubbed his belly. "But I think I might have eaten too much."

"Well that's a shame as I've made Queen of Puddings for dessert."

"Oh... well I suppose there's a small space left." Rick smiled. "What do you say kids?"

"Yessss!" they replied in unison.

Jackie's desserts were legendary and when she had a chance, she took them to the café parties that Allie held. She wasn't always able to attend them because of her work, but when she did, people complimented her on her culinary skills. Before her husband had left, Jackie had always seemed to be smiling and baking. She'd been there to greet her daughters when they got home from school, usually with yummy freshly baked treats for them to enjoy and a hot meal that they sat around and ate together. That all changed after her husband had gone and she'd become withdrawn, depressed and irritable – and that was when she was home – because with the hours she had to work, Dawn and Camilla became latch-key kids. It had been hard returning from school to a cold, empty house, with no delicious aromas of cakes, biscuits or cottage pie greeting them. So Dawn knew how awful life could be if a couple split up, for them and for their children. And she had carried the fear of being betrayed and divorced throughout her life. Her mother's little reminders of how men could leave didn't help at all, although she understood why Jackie worried. It was natural for a mother to worry, after all.

Jackie got up to take the plates out but Rick held up a hand. "I'll do this. You and my gorgeous wife have done enough."

He stacked the dinner plates then carried them from the dining room.

"Laura and James, if you look in the cupboard there, you'll find the small bowls." Jackie gestured at the Welsh dresser.

"I'll go and help Rick. He probably can't locate the spoons, knowing him." Dawn got up and went through to the kitchen but Rick wasn't there. She paused and listened. Perhaps he'd gone to the toilet.

Then she heard the low tones of his voice and looked through the window. He was out there, on his mobile phone, his cheeks flushed as he listened and nodded. She gripped the edge of the sink and watched him. Who was he talking to? He'd agreed not to take calls on a Sunday, as in the past, he'd been called into work on several occasions, and it always hurt Dawn to see him hurrying away when he should be spending time with his family.

He said something sharply, then ended the call and stuffed his mobile back into his pocket. A muscle in his jaw twitched as he stared blankly at the fence dividing Jackie's garden from her neighbour's. He looked so far away, so removed from the energetic, light-hearted man she'd met all those years ago at university. Back then, they'd had so much fun together. They'd both been young, hopeful, enthusiastic about life and what lay ahead of them, and had spent so many hours talking, planning, sharing their hopes and dreams, making love into the small hours of the morning and collapsing into bed as the dawn light flooded the sky.

She'd been certain back then that this was the man for her, that he loved her as much as she loved him and that they'd always be together.

But that was then.

And this was now.

Rick was slipping through her fingers like sand in an egg timer, and she hadn't the foggiest idea how to stop him.

As Jackie served the Queen of Puddings, Rick clapped his hands together.

"Laura and James, we have a very special announcement!"

The children dragged their eyes from the dessert to look at their parents. Dawn shifted on her chair. Rick took her hand and kissed it.

"You are going to have a little baby sister or brother."

A tiny line appeared between Laura's brows. "A baby?"

"Yes. In about five months, give or take a week or two."

Dawn suppressed a nervous giggle. Rick was always so careful with numbers, even with this news. And perhaps he was right to be. After all, Laura had arrived a week later than her due date and James had arrived two weeks before his. So expected dates of delivery were not necessarily precise, and with the children, they needed to ensure that they weren't expecting the baby to arrive right on time. Laura had a thing about times anyway, especially since Rick's working hours had increased again, and she would no doubt mark the baby's EDD on the rabbit calendar that hung on her bedroom wall and tick off the days as they passed.

"I want a brother." James nodded as he accepted a bowl of dessert from his nanna.

"You can't decide what you're having, James." Laura scowled at him. "It just happens."

"But I don't want a sister." His bottom lip wobbled. "I have you."

Laura patted her brother's hand. "I will always be your sister but you might have another one. Isn't that right, Daddy?"

"That's right, sweetheart. So are we pleased?"

Laura nodded and James shrugged, so that would have to do for now. It was a lot for them to take in, but they'd have time now to get used to the idea. Dawn hadn't wanted to tell them until the pregnancy was well established, because it would have been dreadful if they'd known, then she'd lost the baby. Of course, nothing was 100 per cent certain and things could still go wrong, but she was well past the three-month danger point, and had quite a bump already, so they had to tell them sooner or later. It was getting too hard to hide her belly all the time anyway.

"Here you are, Dawn."

Her mother handed her a bowl and she took it then gazed at its contents. Growing up, Queen of Puddings had always been one of her favourites with its layers of light fluffy sponge, custard and jam, topped with soft, chewy meringue. But right now, she didn't fancy it at all.

All she did fancy was cuddling up with her husband and having him stroke her hair as he told her how much he loved her and the children and how he'd never leave them. But he was currently tucking into his dessert, seemingly oblivious to her vulnerability, and blissfully unaware that she'd seen him on his phone outside, lost in conversation with someone who brought a colour to his cheeks that Dawn didn't think she'd seen in quite some time.

5

*D*awn set up the ironing board in the quiet house. Rick had left at six-thirty, as he always did on Monday mornings, and the children were in school. She usually liked this time of day, when she could put the radio on in the sunny kitchen, make a cup of tea and read a magazine or a book, get some chores done or just sit and think.

She'd been out to check on Wallace the second and Lulu, and had found them quietly nibbling on hay, so she'd given them some carrots, changed the water in the bottle that clipped to the front of the hutch, then gone back inside to switch the kettle on. The new Wallace sure was hefty for a guinea pig. She wondered for a moment what had happened to the other little Wallace. She had asked Rick the previous afternoon, and he'd managed to tell her that he'd found Wallace and brought him home, but then they'd been interrupted by Laura and it had slipped her mind. She was suddenly overwhelmed with guilt and concern, and the only way she could ease it was to blame her pregnancy brain and reassure herself that Rick would have put Wallace somewhere safe. Somewhere the cats from the café couldn't find him, hopefully.

The thermostat on the iron clicked, so she picked a shirt from the ironing pile and slid it over the end of the board. She worked on autopilot: collar, sleeves, side, back, side. She'd done this so many times before that it was automatic, and before she knew it, she'd done four shirts and her tea was getting cold. She poured it down the sink then rinsed the mug.

Something was prickling at her subconscious and she'd been trying to keep it there, out of sight, not wanting to let it surface. But as she gazed at through the kitchen window at the generous garden – where even though it was still warm, the autumnal shades of red, orange and brown dominated – the question shot to the surface like a bubble and popped.

Was her mother right? Was Rick having an affair?

Her hand shot to her mouth. She knew that husbands and wives did cheat; she had her father's behaviour as a prime example. Plus the media loved to parade gritty stories of celebrity marital problems and affairs at the public all the time. She knew people whose marriages had failed because of it and those who'd stayed together, trying to work things out after one of them had cheated, and often they tried to make it work because of their children. But she had never really believed that it could happen in her own marriage. Not between her and Rick; they loved each other, didn't they? They had always sworn that they'd never disrespect each other in that way. But had Rick forgotten that as the years passed? Had someone in his busy, flashy, high-flying City job caught his eye and turned his head while his wife sat at home caring for their two children, getting fatter with her third pregnancy? Was Rick fed up with her or did he want to have some fun then come back to her? Could she allow that?

No she bloody well couldn't.

She took a deep breath. Her thoughts were racing away here and she might be imagining it all. This was Rick she was thinking about. He wouldn't cheat, surely? Not Rick.

She decided to leave the ironing for a bit and to check her Facebook page – that usually made her feel a bit better when worries rushed in. She could see if there was any news from her friends who'd moved away and from the friends she'd made at university. She retrieved the lightweight laptop that she shared with Rick from the study, then took it back to the kitchen, placed it on the kitchen island and switched it on.

It flickered into life and she was about to click on the Internet symbol when a folder caught her eye.

Rick's Stuff.

And her mother's final whispered words from yesterday – the ones she'd uttered into Dawn's ear, just before they left – came rushing back:

"You should check his emails, Dawnie. Just to be sure. It's not right that he's working so late, especially with you being pregnant. I read just last week in one of my magazines that a woman found out her husband was cheating with his secretary – oh the cliché – just from reading his emails. He'd forgotten to close down the account after using the family computer. Check them, then you'll know if there's something going on."

She hovered the mouse over his folder, wondering if she could really do this. It was wrong and she knew that to the bottom of her heart but she also needed to put her mind at rest. And Rick was at work, probably wouldn't be home until late. If she did this, she could find the much-needed reassurance that she really was being silly.

She opened the folder and found several other blue folders, then clicked on the one labelled *Passwords*.

Bit daft having your passwords stored on here, Rick.

But then he had so many and was constantly having to change them as he'd forgotten them, so it seemed he'd decided to keep them all in one place. There were probably lots of people who did the same thing, in spite of the warnings about cyber security and hackers.

The folder opened and she found a six-page Word document with the names of accounts and the passwords next to them. She scanned down the pages, her heart beating hard and a sour taste filling her mouth. Because she knew this was wrong. Rick obviously didn't have anything to hide but then he wouldn't expect her to go snooping. He'd actually told her at one point that he'd made a list of all his accounts, just in case anything ever happened to him and she needed to access them. It would make things easier, he'd said. She'd tried to laugh it off, not wanting to think about the possibility of being without Rick, but he'd been true to his word and ensured that she'd know where everything was if she needed it.

Her eyes stopped on the heading *Rick's email account*.

She shouldn't really, but she could just take a peek then be done with all this worrying.

Before she could overthink it, she clicked on the Internet link and signed into the account with the password.

The first few emails were from the bank and PayPal. The next was from an online sports company that was headed FLASH SALE: 50% off selected lines today only. The next one looked more interesting. More worrying. It was from a Brianna Mandrell and the subject heading was FYEO.

FYEO?

Dawn's heart raced as she realised what that meant.

For your eyes only.

What the hell?

Her finger shook above the touchpad.

Her mind was screaming at her to stop; it was better not to know.

But...

She had to know.

She opened it.

And immediately wished she hadn't.

Dawn hurried up the path to The Cosy Cottage Café. She opened the door with such force that she nearly faceplanted onto the welcome mat. She steadied herself then glanced around. Five customers: two women, two male delivery drivers and Fred Bennett, an elderly man from the village who always came to the café on a Monday morning.

She couldn't see Allie, so she must be in the kitchen.

She went to the counter and stood there waiting, suddenly aware that she must look quite a state. After dropping the children at school, she'd changed into a pair of Rick's old lounge pants and a washed out black t-shirt. Comfortable clothes for wearing while ironing. After seeing that terrible email, she hadn't bothered to change. Her hair was in a messy ponytail and in her hurry to get to the café, the fringe she'd been growing out had slipped from its clip and now stuck to her clammy forehead. And as for makeup... she hadn't bothered with that. Who was going to see her at home? What did it matter anyway?

Allie didn't appear, so Dawn went behind the counter and into the kitchen. She found her friend scooping poached eggs from a pan then carefully arranging them on top of thick slices of toast covered with mashed avocado.

"Dawn! You gave me a fright then." Allie paused, an egg suspended on the spatula in mid air, its golden yolk shiny and perfectly round, just waiting to be pierced by a fork. Dawn's stomach rolled.

"Sorry. I had to come to see you. I can't go to Mum's as she'll be doing her cleaning rounds and Camilla's in work and I didn't know who else to go to and..."

Allie's expression changed as she took in Dawn's appearance.

"Hold on." She laid the egg on a slice toast then put the saucepan on the worktop. "Now, do you want to take a deep breath then tell me what's going on? I love you, Dawnie, and you can always come to me when you need to but to be quite frank, you look like you've been dragged through a hedge backwards."

Dawn took a breath and was dismayed to find her vision blurring. Her throat ached as a lump rose there and she tried to speak but it emerged as a squeak.

"Okay, you stay here. I have to take these breakfasts out but I'll be right back." Allie dusted her hands on her apron then pushed Dawn onto a stool that she'd pulled from under the kitchen island, before disappearing with two plates.

Dawn took the time to try to pull herself together. Allie was always so kind and caring that whenever Dawn was feeling emotional, her composure usually slipped. She'd always worn her heart on her sleeve and her mother had often remarked that she was very different to Camilla in that respect. After their father had left, Camilla had seemed to toughen up, taking care of Dawn and their mother like they were her responsibility, even though she'd only been ten. Jackie had fallen into a deep depression and ten-year-old Camilla had taken over the running of the house while Jackie was out at work, ensuring that she and Dawn had clean uniforms and got to school on time. Camilla had made excuses to her teachers when her mother hadn't shown up for parents' evenings and had used her saved pocket money to purchase tins of beans and loaves of bread from the local shop to feed them. Jackie had emerged from the worst of her darkness after about eight months, but it had been an awful time.

Camilla had been a rock. But it was as if the whole experience had left her scarred and scared. She'd never had a long-term relationship and very rarely ever let her guard down, not even to Dawn. Her decision to never have children had been one that had initially shocked Dawn, as she'd longed to be a mother after falling in love with Rick. However, as time went on and Camilla didn't falter in her decision, not even when she held her niece and nephew as tiny babies, Dawn realised that it was okay for her sister to lack maternal yearnings. As long Camilla was happy with her life, then Dawn didn't need to worry about her. Sometimes, she even envied Camilla her freedom, her lack of responsibility, the fact that she could go into London and splurge on clothes and shoes then stay in a luxury hotel without worrying about the price or getting back for the school run. She wondered what it would be like to have a full night's sleep and to spend an hour lounging in a bubble bath without someone needing the toilet, or a drink, or having a fight over the TV remote.

But their lives were very different and their parents' divorce had affected them in different ways. Camilla swore she never wanted the whole marriage and children scenario while Dawn couldn't imagine not having that life that she treasured. If anything, seeing her mother's breakdown made Dawn crave domesticity. Her childhood had seemed perfect until her father left and in the weeks that followed his departure, she'd longed to come home from school to find her mother baking again, ready with a kiss and a smile at the door. But that idyllic stage of her life had passed and it never returned. Until Dawn married Rick and had her own home, and became determined to have the perfect family life, to be the wife and mother that Jackie had been before her husband had left. It was like she had a chance to recreate the early part of her childhood – the part that she'd enjoyed.

And now it seemed that it was falling apart, in spite of all her efforts.

"Right, Mrs," Allie was back with a steaming mug and a ginger biscuit, "I want you to take these then come and sit on my leather couch and tell me all about it."

"Thank you, Allie."

"No need to thank me, sweetheart. I'm your friend and that's what friends do. You need to tell me what's weighing you down and got you running around the village looking like you spent the night sleeping rough."

Dawn tugged at the t-shirt, trying to stop it clinging to her belly.

"Okay... but I have a feeling that you're not going to approve of what I've done."

Allie placed a hand on Dawn's back then gently ushered her from the kitchen.

"I am quite sure that you can't possibly have done anything terrible, Dawn."

Dawn swallowed a sob.

Because she was quite sure that as soon as she told Allie what she had done, her friend was going to change her mind.

Just as Dawn was about to tell Allie about the email, Camilla breezed into the café. As usual, she looked gorgeous with her dark elfin crop, her dazzling green eyes enhanced with shimmering emerald makeup and her designer charcoal-grey trouser suit and purple silk blouse. Her towering heels clicked across the floor as she made her way to the counter, then she caught sight of Allie and Dawn and did an about turn to join them at the sofa.

"Camilla, what're you doing here?" Dawn blurted.

"Well that's a nice welcome."

"I didn't mean it like that. What I meant was, why aren't you in London?"

"Oh, I had a meeting with a local client then I thought I'd pop in for a coffee. Didn't expect to see you here either little sister." Camilla peered at her. "Have you been crying?"

Dawn shifted on the sofa.

"She's a bit hormonal." Allie patted Dawn's hand.

"Yes it all gets a bit much sometimes."

"Shall I pop you to the surgery? See if we can get your GP to take a look at you? Perhaps you need some iron tablets or something else…" Camilla's eyes were wary now, full of sisterly concern.

"No, no. I'm all right. No need for that."

"Would you like a coffee, Camilla?" Allie asked.

"Yes, please, Allie, that would be lovely. Then I think we three need to have a chat."

While Allie made the coffee, Camilla excused herself and popped to the toilet. Dawn took the chance to catch her breath. Part of her didn't want to tell her friend or her sister about Rick, because she didn't want to prejudice their feelings towards him, but part of her wanted, and needed, their support. How dare he do what it seemed like he'd been doing? If he had been doing anything at all. If only she could know for sure.

Soon, Camilla sat opposite her and Allie next to her.

"Um… please don't judge me, but I've done something and it's opened a can of worms."

They both stared at her, their expressions unreadable as they waited for her to continue.

"I've had some suspicions about Rick for a while now and this morning, I just had to find out if they were true."

"What suspicions?" Camilla asked as she shrugged out of her jacket then draped it over the back of the chair.

"That he might be cheating." She pressed her lips together as Camilla's eyes widened.

"What?"

"Oh Dawn, but why?" Allie took her hand.

"He's been acting differently. Since before this pregnancy actually, although it has got worse. Or perhaps it's just me being paranoid and—"

"Dawn! Stop blaming yourself and tell us what's going on." Camilla frowned.

Okay…" She sighed. "He works long hours, repeatedly claims his trains have been delayed and has more events in the City than ever."

"But he works in investment banking. The demands are the same as they've always been but he's now competing with younger and probably more ambitious colleagues. It's a cut-throat career. You knew this when you married him and you said you could deal with it."

"Don't judge me, Camilla."

"No... I'm not judging you, darling. I'm just trying to understand what's going on here. If he is cheating then I'll kill him but you have to be sure. If you accuse him of this it could destroy your marriage and your life... your children's lives."

"Don't you think I know that?" Dawn's voice cracked. "Sorry, I don't mean to sound defensive. I just hate this. I mean... I love him so much but I can't deny that things have changed."

"What evidence do you have that he's been cheating?" Allie asked.

"He's been getting calls and text messages at funny times. And I know it could be colleagues and clients but I just have a gut feeling that it isn't. At least not all of them."

Camilla crossed her legs and drummed her fingers on her kneecap. "But that's still not sufficient evidence to convict the man of adultery."

"I went into his email account this morning."

Camilla sucked in a sharp breath through her teeth. "Oh dear."

Dawn held up her hands. "I shouldn't have and I feel dreadful for it. Snooping is the worst but I had to know."

"What did you find?" Allie's tone was soft and inviting confidence.

"An email titled FYEO."

"FYEO?" Allie shook her head.

"For your eyes only." Camilla explained. "Did you read it?"

"Yes, Camilla. Of course I did."

"And?"

"It seems that my husband has been arranging a weekend away at a luxury spa with some woman called Brianna Mandrell." Even saying the name out loud made her feel queasy.

"Oh."

"Oh? Camilla, I thought you'd be furious."

Her sister sighed. "Look, Dawn, maybe it's not what it seems like. Maybe it's—"

"It does sound a bit suspicious, Camilla." Allie chewed her lip. "I'd certainly advise speaking to him about this as soon as possible, Dawn. Just to clear it up."

"But if I do that, he'll know I've been snooping. He'll never trust me again. I mean... I've turned into a completely paranoid, emotional, swollen, pregnant snooper." She huffed and covered her face with her hands.

"Insecurity can drive us to do things we wouldn't normally consider doing." Allie rubbed Dawn's back. "But this really would be best out in the open."

"I know." Dawn muttered into her palms.

"Or perhaps not."

Dawn lowered her hands and met Camilla's eyes.

"You think I shouldn't say anything?"

"I just think you should give Rick a chance here. You know... he could have a perfectly good reason for this email and for all the other things that are worrying you. Why don't I have a word with him?"

"That's probably not a good idea. But thank you anyway."

"I could do it from a sisterly perspective. If you do it, you'll get emotional, but if I do it, I can keep calm and find out the truth."

"I don't know, Camilla."

"Give me one chance. I'll be careful how I say it. I'll just... elicit the facts."

Dawn looked from Allie to her sister then at her hands where they sat in her lap. Her nails hadn't received any attention in ages and the cuticles were ragged from where she'd chewed them. And as for her hands; they were red and chapped from where she'd washed them repeatedly then failed to moisturise them. She just didn't have time for such self-care anymore. Had Rick gone off her because she didn't make enough effort?

"I think I should try first, Camilla. I don't want to make things worse."

"Up to you, sweetheart. But I'm willing to talk to him if you want me to."

"Thanks. Right... I'm going to get my nails done."

"What? Now?"

"Yes. I haven't had them done in a lifetime. I'm going to see if Jenny can fit me in at the salon."

"I'll come with you." Camilla started to rise.

"No, please don't. I need some time to think." Dawn stood up. "Thanks, Allie. Speak to you later, Camilla."

She opened the door to the café then turned to wave at her friend and her sister, but Camilla had already taken Dawn's seat on the sofa and was deep in conversation with Allie. She glanced up and flushed when she spotted Dawn watching her.

Was something going on with Camilla too, or was she expressing her concerns at Dawn's behaviour?

Dawn shook her head then left the café, wondering how she was going to get through the next few months, but hoping that a manicure might be a good place to start.

6

Sitting in the stylish salon, Dawn tried to focus on what Jenny was saying, but her mind was jumping around from one scenario to another.

"What was that?" Dawn asked. "Sorry, Jenny, it's pregnancy brain."

"Oh, so you are pregnant?"

"Yes. I take it you had your suspicions then?"

Jenny shrugged. "Could've been that you'd put a few pounds on, so I'd never have said anything."

"A few pounds?" Dawn lowered her eyes to her belly. "We were going to tell people soon, make it all official, but we wanted to tell the children first."

"Well congratulations! That's fabulous news."

Jenny watched Dawn's face.

"Isn't it?"

"It is. Fabulous." Dawn sighed. "It was just a bit of a shock."

"Not all babies are planned but they bring the love with them. Isn't that how the saying goes. At least, it's something like that. Anyway, good for you. I've always thought of you and Rick as the perfect couple. You seem so happy and so perfectly matched."

Dawn bit the inside of her cheek. Was that how others saw her and Rick? As perfect? If only they knew the truth. She swallowed hard, trying to dislodge the painful lump that had lodged in her throat.

"Thank you. That's a very kind thing to say."

Jenny smiled then looked down at Dawn's nails again. "There you go. That looks much better doesn't it?"

Dawn admired the shimmering lilac polish that Jenny had applied to her nails. Her cuticles were now neat and her hands looked much better because Jenny had soaked them, exfoliated them, then smoothed in a rich rose scented lotion that made Dawn think of Turkish delight.

"Tell you what, shall I do you a pedicure too? On the house?"

"That would be lovely. But I'm happy to pay."

"Won't hear of it. My way of saying congratulations." Jenny shook her head and her long blue hair fell over her shoulders. Dawn found it hard to keep up with the stylist's changing hair colour, just last week it had been dyed different shades of grey and now it was a rich azure blue that reminded Dawn think of foreign summer skies.

"Well, thank you. But I do need to pop to the toilet first."

"Of course."

Dawn got up and made her way to the back of the salon then went through the black door and into the toilets.

Ten minutes later, she emerged.

"If you want to take a seat here, Dawn, I'll soak your feet in…" Jenny stopped mid sentence. "Dawn?"

She hurried over and took hold of Dawn's arms. "What is it? You've gone white as a sheet."

Dawn opened her mouth to explain but the dull ache in her abdomen caused her to hunch over with fear.

"It's all right, lovely, just sit down. Everything will be okay."

But as Jenny lowered her into a chair, everything went black.

The sound of whispering dragged Dawn from the warm, dark place where she'd been floating. The whispers sounded familiar and she knew, deep inside, that she had to surface.

But it was so nice in the darkness where she was weightless and didn't have to worry about anything.

Except for Laura and James!

She needed to pick her children up from school.

She opened her eyes and sat up quickly.

"Dawn?"

Rick leaned over her, his face pale and his eyes pools of concern.

"Dawn, lie back down."

"What? Where are Laura and James? I need to get them from school."

"No you don't. Your mother's going to pick them up today and give them dinner. Dawn you're in hospital. I came as quickly as I could. Camilla rang me. She said… she said that you'd collapsed at Jenny's salon and that Jenny called an ambulance then called her."

As Dawn settled back on the pillow in its white starched hospital-issue pillowcase, it all came flooding back. She'd had her nails done then gone to the toilet. She'd discovered blood in her underwear. She'd gone back out to tell Jenny then felt all woozy and... that was all she remembered. Except for being in an ambulance with a very kind female paramedic then being wheeled into the hospital and into a room where she'd been told to rest while they organised tests and a scan.

"But I only fainted. I didn't need to come here."

"They were concerned because you blacked out and because of the bleeding. Jenny was in a right old state apparently."

"Poor Jenny."

"Poor *you*!" He took her hand as he perched on the side of the bed. "I don't know how I'd manage if anything ever happened to you, Dawn."

"The baby?" She touched her stomach.

He shook his head.

"No!"

"They don't know what's wrong yet. That's why they want to scan you. They said... they said..." He sighed then rubbed his eyes. "They said bleeding before twenty-four weeks is viewed as a threatened miscarriage but it could all be fine. The baby might be okay. Apparently, there are lots of reasons for bleeding in pregnancy."

"But I fainted."

He nodded. "That could well be the shock of seeing the blood, and according to the paramedic, your blood pressure is quite low again."

Dawn's heart melted as she took in how distressed he was. His tie was askew, his shirt crumpled and the fine lines around his eyes seemed deeper, as if the morning's events had aged him rapidly.

Whatever might be different between them, he did care, and that made her want to hug him.

"Come here." She opened her arms.

Rick leaned forwards and gently embraced her. To be held by him, to breathe in the familiar spicy scent of his aftershave and to bury her face in his neck all made her want everything to be okay again. She couldn't imagine a world where she didn't get to hug him, where she didn't see him every day and know that he was hers.

But she might have to face up to all that if their relationship changed, if his feelings for her had altered as much as she feared.

He released her and she leaned back on the pillows, and he softly stroked her cheek.

"It's all going to be okay, Dawnie. I just know it."

"I hope so, Rick."

But she wasn't just thinking about the baby inside her, she was thinking about her whole life too.

Even though the Early Pregnancy Assessment Unit at the local hospital was extremely busy, they'd managed to fit Dawn in for a scan. Initially, she'd been told she might have to wait until the next day, but there had been a cancellation of a scheduled appointment, so they'd given Dawn the space.

And the baby had been fine. Heart beating strong and limbs moving around, safe in her womb. The relief had been overwhelming and Dawn had been struck by something; even though this baby's conception had not been planned, she did want it. With all of her heart. There was no doubt in her mind.

The medical team had run further tests but admitted that they weren't sure what had caused the bleeding. They'd also reassured her that although it might have seemed as though she'd lost a lot of blood, it was in fact not much at all. Sometimes, bleeding in pregnancy could be down to something as straightforward as changes to the cervix caused by pregnancy hormones, and the dull ache she'd experienced could have been down to those changes. They advised her to take it easy for the next few weeks, although how she was going to manage to do that with two children and a house to run, Dawn had no idea.

"Here's a cuppa, Dawnie," Camilla entered the lounge where Dawn was resting on the sofa. Camilla and Rick had tried to persuade Dawn to stay in bed once they'd arrived home from the hospital, but Dawn had refused. She couldn't bear the thought of being upstairs alone, left to stew with her worries. So Camilla had insisted on bringing the quilt and pillows downstairs, then arranging them on the sofa.

Camilla put the mug on the coffee table then started plumping up the pillows.

"Will you stop?" Dawn swatted her sister's hand away.

"I'm just trying to make you comfy."

"I know and I'm grateful but you don't need to keep fussing and if you keep making me all this tea I won't be able to rest anyway, as I'll be back and fore to the loo."

Camilla nodded then slumped onto the end of the sofa.

"Ouch!" Dawn lurched forwards.

"Dawnie! What is it? More cramps?" Camilla's eyes were wide, her face contorted with worry.

"No, silly, you just sat on my foot."

"Ooops!" Camilla moved to the arm of the sofa and perched there, her eyes restless, her fingers fluttering across her lap.

"Camilla, I'm fine."

"But you're not. Or you weren't. What if you'd lost this

baby? How awful would we all feel then? I'm going to have a word with Rick as soon as—"

"Please don't. He doesn't need to know what I did. Or that I know about the emails and whatever else. Today's scare has helped me re-evaluate. I'm not saying that I condone his... deceit, but I'm hoping there's a good reason for it."

"And there is... I mean, I'm sure there is, but you really need to avoid stress. You can't be worrying that your husband's cheating or going off you or anything else for that matter. You need stability and taking care of."

"I know. But I'll speak to Rick in my own time." Dawn tilted her head. "Where is he anyway?"

"Upstairs."

"He's been gone for ages."

"I think he's on the phone." Camilla's eyes widened at her own words. "It's probably just work."

Dawn slumped onto the pillows. "Probably."

Rick had rushed back to be at Dawn's side then insisted that he'd stay home for the rest of the week, so he probably did have things he needed to sort out. She hoped it wouldn't get him into trouble; she knew his bosses didn't like their employees missing time. But surely this was a good reason to take some compassionate leave or even to work from home?

The next morning, Dawn sat in bed fighting the urge to get up and go downstairs to see what was going on. So far, in the forty-five minutes since Rick had got the children up, she'd heard Rick swearing, Laura reprimanding her father and James crying. She could smell burnt toast and the tea Rick had brought her, which was rapidly cooling on her bedside table, tasted faintly of washing-up liquid. It seemed like everything that could go wrong had gone wrong.

But Rick had told her to stay in bed and that under no circumstances was she to get up until the children had left for school. When she'd gone to the toilet first thing, she'd seen traces of blood, so she knew she had to listen, but there was less than yesterday.

She was also trying not to worry, because stressing wasn't going to help.

About the baby and about Rick. He'd been so loving and attentive since he'd brought her home, and she was even wondering if she'd imagined the email. Had she dreamt it, perhaps? Or read things into it that weren't really there? Was she being oversensitive?

She decided to push it from her mind and to focus on resting and enjoying the week with Rick. It wasn't often that they had time alone together, without the children around, and it would be nice to have that quality time. Perhaps this time alone would strengthen their relationship and prepare them for their new addition.

Footsteps on the stairs alerted her to an approaching child.

"Muu-uum!" It was James.

"Morning, angel."

He ran at the bed and flung himself onto her just as Rick stormed into the room.

"James! Don't run at your mum like that. Remember what we spoke about?"

James gently moved off Dawn and nodded, his cheeks blushing scarlet.

"You said we have to be good and gentle with Mummy because she's not very well."

"That's right."

"Oh James, I'm not ill but I do need to rest because I'm growing a baby."

She didn't want her son worrying about her being ill. A girl in his class at school had lost her mother to breast cancer the previous year and she'd seen the terror in James's eyes when he'd heard about it. He was a worrier and she couldn't bear to think about him wondering when he'd lose her.

"But you'll be okay now?" he asked, his eyes wide.

"Yes, James, I'll be okay."

She opened her arms and he crawled up the bed to sit next to her, then carefully snuggled into her.

"Is he all right there?" Rick asked.

"Yes, he's fine. Everything okay downstairs?"

Rick winked at her. "Running like clockwork." Then he mock wiped his brow. "I have to be honest, I don't know how you make it look so easy."

"Do you need me to come down?"

"Absolutely not! You have a cuddle with James. I'll go and—"

"Daddy, are you going to get us a new toaster?"

"What?" Dawn raised her eyebrows.

"Nothing to worry about. I just burnt a piece of toast then it got jammed in the toaster so I shook it and now it won't work."

Dawn suppressed laughter. "We needed a new one anyway."

"We certainly do... now. Right, see you in a bit. James, make sure you let Mummy rest."

"Yes, Daddy."

Dawn held her son in her arms and sighed with contentment. He might be six but he was still her baby. She buried her head in his hair and breathed in the scent of apple shampoo. His hair was soft and fine. She wondered if the new baby would look like her, or if he or she would be another mini-Rick. It was exciting to think that soon there would be another person joining them, another child for her to love. After she'd given birth to Laura, she'd fallen so much in love with her that she hadn't thought she could ever have room in her heart to love another child as much. Then James had arrived and she'd loved him equally. Maternal love wasn't limited and she had plenty to share with three children.

"Mummy?" James leaned backwards to meet her eyes.
"Yes?"
"Can the baby hear me?"
"Yes, darling. At least I think so."

He pressed his mouth against her belly. "Baby, I'm your big brother, James. Now don't you come out until it's time or you'll be too small. When you do come I will look after you. I promise."

Dawn's eyes filled with tears at his sweet words.

Then she felt a fluttering in her belly, like bubbles popping and she gasped.

"What's wrong, Mummy?"
"The baby just moved."
"For me?"
"Yes, James, I think it's because you spoke to him or her."

She'd felt some movement over the past few weeks but hadn't been sure if it was the baby or wind, and hadn't made a fuss because the children still hadn't known about the pregnancy.

He grinned.
"Mummy?"
"Yes, angel."

"How did the baby get in there?"

Dawn choked as laughter burst from her chest. She looked around, as if she could find an appropriate answer for a six-year-old, then at a loss, she grabbed the mug of tea and winced as she swallowed a sour mouthful.

"Now that's an interesting question, James."

He watched her, his big eyes wide and interested.

"Tell you what, why don't you ask your father?"

James nodded then snuggled back into her, and Dawn bit her lip as she imagined Rick's face when his son asked him that age-old question. She hoped he'd have a good answer ready and knew that she'd want to be there to listen when James asked.

7

Over the next few days, Dawn tried to rest. It was difficult when she saw Rick struggling with things and she had to stop herself taking over. He did try really hard but he wasn't used to the domestic side of things around the house as Dawn had always done them. It had worked for them because Dawn had wanted it to. Rick did the traditionally male things and Dawn did the housework and chores; it was the way it had been since she'd given up her teaching post after having James. And, of course, her desire for the more traditional family lay rooted in her past and her yearning for the stability and happiness she'd enjoyed as a young child. Besides which, by the time Rick got home in the evenings, he was usually so tired that she didn't have the heart to ask him to run the vacuum round or to do the ironing, and on weekends she wanted him to spend quality time with the children.

She realised now though, that something would need to change, because with a new baby on the way, she wouldn't be able to do everything that she had been doing.

But this week, as she'd lain on the sofa watching daytime

TV, Rick had managed to wash a black sock with the whites, which had made them all grey. Then he'd shrunk one of her favourite cashmere (hand-wash only) cardigans by putting it on a boil wash. He'd put frozen chips in the oven to go with fried eggs, but forgotten to turn the oven on, so when the eggs were ready, the chips were still ice-cold. He'd been ironing his work shirts and answered a call on his mobile, leaving the iron face down on a shirt and burned a hole in it. And he'd gone food shopping and spent three times Dawn's usual budget by picking up the first version of everything on the list she'd written, and not searching around for the best value products like Dawn did.

But he'd been trying so hard and she loved him for it, and, she could see that he was learning fast. His latest attempt at ironing had been very impressive, especially as he'd done it while Skyping a client. The camera on his laptop had been positioned so that only his head was visible though, so he didn't seem unprofessional. Then he'd boiled all the whites he'd dyed grey and returned them – almost – to their former condition.

As for Dawn herself, she was feeling much better, and thankfully the bleeding had stopped. She wasn't out of the woods yet but a few more days and she felt sure she'd be able to resume some of her normal tasks, just slowly.

Friday had arrived, the children were at school, and Rick had insisted that she have a lie in and breakfast in bed. He'd toasted her crumpets, in the new toaster, and served them with real butter and some of the homemade strawberry jam that Allie had given them recently, insisting that she had a surplus after the summer. He'd brought her a big mug of tea and a glass of freshly squeezed orange juice too. As she ate, he sat next to her on the bed and read the paper on his tablet.

"This is nice." She dabbed her mouth with the paper napkin.

Rick turned to her. "It is, isn't it?"

Their bedroom was warm with autumn sunshine and outside, the breeze toyed with the few remaining leaves of the silver birch in their front garden.

"I love the autumn."

"I know you do."

"It reminds me of our New York trip."

"Back in our youth?" He grinned.

"Well, we were young, yes."

"What and we're ancient now?"

"No, but... well things change don't they? And we were only in our twenties when we went out there. It was such a great week. I wish..." She bit her lip. She was about to say that she wished they could go again and be like they used to, but that wasn't going to happen for a while, not with a new baby and two young children.

"What do you wish?"

"Oh it doesn't matter."

He placed his tablet on the bedside table and turned around to face her properly. "Tell me."

"I just miss how good things used to be between us. Back when it was fresh and new and exciting."

"And when we weren't sleep-deprived and trying to do a million things while feeling guilty about the things we're not doing."

"Yes. It's hard sometimes. I love Laura and James... they're my world. Our world. But I miss just being with you."

Rick took her hand. "I love you, you know."

"I love you too." She sighed. "And I feel guilty now for wishing for things when I have so much to be grateful for."

"You should never feel guilty. And I miss having more time with you too. But I do love our life and our children and even though sometimes it's so hard I could sleep standing up; I still wouldn't change a thing. Well... except for..." He shook his head.

"Except for what? Rick?"

"Nothing. Nothing at all, my beautiful wife. I'm just a bit tired. Right then... how about you take a nice long shower then smother yourself in that luxurious – and very expensive – moisturiser that the children bought you for Mother's Day?"

"Okay." Dawn wanted to ask him again what he was going to say but it was clear that he wanted to move the conversation on.

"I'll take your breakfast things down and make the sofa up for you."

"Rick, I think I can manage without a quilt on the sofa today."

He frowned.

"Perhaps. But you still have to take it easy."

She nodded.

"I have a little surprise arriving later that I'm hoping you're going to enjoy."

So he was planning surprises for her. That must mean that nothing was wrong and that he hadn't been about to tell her something to upset her. She was being too sensitive again.

So she would forget that Rick had said *except for...* and get on with her day. It would be their last full day alone together anyway, as the children would be home over the weekend, then Rick had to go back to work on Monday. Exactly how she'd manage then, she wasn't quite sure but she'd cross that bridge when she came to it.

She pushed back the quilt and slid her legs over the edge of the bed and wondered exactly what surprise it was that Rick had planned for her.

Dawn descended the stairs quietly. She was sure she'd heard voices when she'd got out of the shower. She had moisturised then dressed as quickly as she could without getting moisturiser all over her clothes. Her regular jeans were all too tight now, so she'd pulled on a pair of grey linen trousers with an elasticated waist and a loose black tunic top.

At the bottom of the stairs, she paused. She could definitely hear Rick speaking to someone. Her heart jolted. Was he on the phone again?

She marched into the kitchen, about to give him a piece of her mind, but found Allie at the kitchen table unloading a large basket.

"Allie!"

Her friend turned and smiled.

"Hey, sweetheart. How're you feeling?"

"Better. Yes, much better, thanks. What are you doing here? Gosh... that sounded terribly rude and I didn't mean it like that. I was just surprised."

Allie laughed. "Well that's for Rick to explain."

Allie turned to her husband.

"This is your surprise. I asked Allie if she'd have time to prepare us a nice lunch for today, seeing as how it'll be our last bit of peace and quiet for a while."

"You weren't too busy?" Dawn asked Allie as she took in the number of foil containers and various bowls on the table.

"Of course not. I mean, we're always busy but Jordan is

working today and he's enlisted Max to help him out. Which freed me up to do this for you."

"That's so kind of you." Dawn smiled.

"Rick is paying me for it, so..." Allie's cheeks coloured.

"I bloody well hope he is. You have a business to run, you can't keep giving stuff away, you know."

Dawn crossed the room then gave her friend a hug.

"And Rick... This is so thoughtful of you. Thank you so much."

The aromas coming from the table were making her mouth water, even though she hadn't long had breakfast.

"I must be getting better. My appetite seems to be returning with a vengeance."

Rick came and stood next to her then slid his arm around her waist.

"I'm glad to hear it. I've been so worried about you."

He kissed the top of her head and she leaned into him.

"I think everything you need is there, Rick. I've written down some warming instructions, although everything can be eaten cold if you prefer. Oh, and I'll just pop the ice cream in the freezer."

"Thanks, Allie."

"And you're all sorted for collecting the children from school today?"

"Yes, I'll get them. I'm quite enjoying being able to do the school run. It's amazing what you miss out on because of work."

Allie nodded.

"I'll see you out then."

Rick escorted Allie to the door and Dawn eyed the food on the table. It was still early, so they couldn't enjoy it yet, but it was certainly a lovely surprise.

"What time do you want to eat, my gorgeous wife?" Rick

entered the kitchen. "I don't know about you but I won't be able to wait too long."

"I'm so glad you said that. Shall we give it an hour though?"

"An hour maximum."

"What do you want to do now?" Dawn peered up at him, taking in his strong jaw, his broad shoulders and his slim hips. Something stirred inside her that she hadn't felt in quite some time.

Rick stepped closer and cupped her face. "I know what I'd like to do but I don't think it's wise right now."

Dawn leaned her head against his chest, breathing in his delicious scent.

"I know, you're right. We probably shouldn't."

He lifted her chin and gazed into her eyes. "It's not that I don't want to, because I really, really do. I love you, Dawnie, and desire you more than you could imagine. But I would be too worried because of what happened."

"Me too."

She closed her eyes as he gently kissed her lips.

"How about a head massage instead while we watch some daytime TV?"

"With a cuppa?"

"Now you're talking. You go and switch the TV on and I'll boil the kettle."

Dawn nodded then left the kitchen, her body conflicted between desire for her husband and a maternal need to protect her unborn baby. But her heart felt lighter than it had done for weeks.

Because Rick had told her that he loved and desired her and was trying to show her that in a variety of ways. So daytime TV and a cup of tea would have to be a substitute for passionate lovemaking – for the next few months, at least.

Dawn moaned with pleasure as Rick gently massaged her head. He was sitting behind her on the sofa with her head resting on his chest. He ran his fingers through her hair then rubbed her temples and worked his hands backwards to behind her ears.

When he stopped, she was weak and completely relaxed.

Then there was a knock at the door, so Rick slid out from behind her and went to answer it. Dawn strained to listen but Rick soon returned, holding a large box.

"What's that?"

"Get your shoes on and come out the back garden with me."

"What? Why?"

"There's something we need to do."

Dawn fetched her shoes then followed Rick outside. He carried the box down to the bottom of the garden then set it in front of the flowerbed.

There was a slightly raised mound of earth there and she let out a sigh. "I'd forgotten to ask if you'd had a chance to bury him."

"Yes I brought him out here because I thought you'd want him to stay at home. He's all wrapped up in a shoebox and I dug quite a deep hole, so there's no chance of anything... you know..."

"Digging him up?" Dawn's bottom lip wobbled. "Poor Wallace."

"Hey, don't get upset. He had a good life."

"But he was so young."

"He was but he could have had a medical condition we didn't know about."

Dawn nodded. "It's still sad though."

"And part of life. But at least he's home again."

"I know. If you hadn't found him, it would have been awful."

"A giant white rat!" Rick shook his head.

"I bet it did give Mrs Burnley quite a fright. So what's in the box?"

"I thought we should have some way of marking this spot. And one day, when the children are a bit older, we can tell them the truth about Wallace."

"If they don't already suspect. Laura's quite sharp, you know."

He smiled. "Don't I know it? You should've heard her bossing me around this week in the mornings."

"I did, don't worry. She doesn't miss much."

"She certainly doesn't."

Rick opened the box and lifted out a bare root rose that sat in a small plastic container. "It'll need to soak in water for at least two hours then I can plant it here."

"Let me guess... the roses will be white?"

"Of course."

"Thank you." Dawn's vision blurred and she blinked rapidly.

"Don't thank me. This is what we do, Dawnie. We support each other and look after each other and our family."

He wrapped his arms around her and held her tight, and she relaxed against him, knowing there was no place she'd rather be.

"Have you tried the couscous yet?" Rick gestured at Dawn's plate with his fork.

"No." She lifted a forkful to her mouth. "Mmmmm."

"How good is that?"

"Delicious."

They were sitting at the kitchen table, tucking into the food Allie had delivered. And what a feast it was: small cheese and sundried tomato tartlets, roast-vegetable couscous with a basil olive-oil drizzle, green-lentil tabbouleh, asparagus, spinach and halloumi salad, chicken panzanella and for dessert, a large cherry pie and homemade coconut ice cream.

Allie had also provided a bottle of cloudy elderflower lemonade, that was sweet, refreshing and zesty and went perfectly with the food.

"This has been a wonderful day, Rick." Dawn raised her glass. "To family."

"To our wonderful family and to you for growing our baby."

They clinked glasses.

Ten minutes later, Dawn looked at the food that was left.

"I don't think we're going to be able to eat all this. I'm stuffed as it is." She gently patted her belly that was straining against her waistband.

"Well the children can enjoy some of it for their tea, can't they?" Rick asked.

"Good idea. Save me... I mean, *you*... cooking."

"Hey, I would've cooked for them anyway. I'm quite enjoying learning."

"I have to try to get back to normal, Rick, I can't lie down forever."

"I know, but not just yet. Besides, I want us to share more of the household chores now, as well as the cooking. I was quite a good cook back when we first got together, but when we bought the house, then had the children, I'm a bit ashamed to admit that we fell into stereotypical roles."

"We did, I know, and that was partly my fault for pushing us into them."

"I didn't put up much of a fight though, did I? I've just been so tired all the time."

"But how is that going to change, Rick?"

He blinked then worried his bottom lip.

"It will. Somehow. Look... we still have the weekend and I have one more surprise for you."

"You do?" Dawn laughed. "But you've spoiled me so much already. What else could you possible have planned?"

He tapped the side of his nose. "You'll know soon enough. Right, I'll get the dishes done then it's time for another cup of tea and an afternoon snooze."

"Ooh, sounds good."

"You can make the tea if you like while I tidy up."

Dawn switched the kettle on while Rick put lids back onto foil containers then placed them into the fridge. He had been so good to her this week and she found it wonderful yet strange, as if she should always be the one doing things. Of course, when her mother had visited earlier in the week, she'd muttered that it wouldn't last. And that had left Dawn biting her tongue as usual. What was it with her mum? Why couldn't she be happy when something nice happened, even if it was on the back of a difficult time? She knew her mother had been hurt and never got over it but still... surely it was time to move on? But then she thought of Camilla and her refusal to fall in love, and knew that for some people, time didn't move on. For some people, it very sadly remained the same.

"What was that sigh for?" Rick asked as he slipped his arms around her waist then leaned his chin on her shoulder.

"I didn't realise I had sighed."

"You did. And it sounded like you're carrying the weight of the world on your shoulders."

"I was just thinking about Mum and Camilla. About why they can't get over what Dad did. It was such a long time ago."

She poured boiling water onto teabags.

"Camilla's okay isn't she?"

"Well, yes. But she's never had a proper relationship and I don't know if she ever will."

"She seems to be enjoying herself."

"Seems... And then there's Mum. Won't look at a man, which is fine, but she also carries so much bitterness around with her."

"I guess she was badly hurt."

"She was, but the way she hangs onto it and constantly bringing it up hurts me too. Sometimes I just want to live life without comparing everything to what my dad did, you know?"

Rick turned her in his arms.

"I do know, Dawnie. It must be hard for you and you are very patient with her."

"I love her and she does so much for me... for us. I can't tell her because it would hurt her and I doubt anything would change."

"Probably not. But perhaps you do need to have a gentle chat about it. Just not at the moment. Wait until you feel stronger."

Dawn nodded. "Perhaps. Anyway, right now I'm going to forget about it and enjoy being with you. We have about two hours until the school run, so let's take our tea upstairs and lounge in bed like we used to when we were students."

"How decadent!" He winked at her. "Going to bed in the afternoon... when it's still light."

He released her then got the milk from the fridge and Dawn poured it into the mugs.

""I never want to feel the way my mother does, Rick."

"You never will, I promise." He picked up the tea. "Come on, let's go lounge."

Dawn followed him out of the kitchen and up the stairs, trying hard to banish all thoughts of the email she'd seen from her mind. Trying to hold her husband's promise there instead, because what was better than his word?

8

Dawn stretched and savoured the delicious tingling in her limbs. She'd had the loveliest nap followed by a refreshing cup of mint tea – that Rick had brought to her in bed before leaving to pick the children up from school. They'd be home soon. She should probably get dressed again. She'd slipped into soft pyjamas for her nap, not wanting to crease her clothes.

The sound of a car entering the street made her sit up. That couldn't be Rick; he'd walked to pick up Laura and James as it would be lazy to drive the five minutes to the school.

She was about to lie back down again when she heard footsteps on the path. Was that Rick? An urge to throw herself into his arms and tell him how much she loved him consumed her. Recently, she'd been beset by so many doubts but the way he'd treated her this week had to show that he loved her, surely?

Dawn reached for her dressing gown and slipped it on then descended the stairs, her heart full of love and happiness. She unlocked the front door then swung it open, about to greet her husband, and she stopped dead. Because the person on her doorstep was not the one she'd been expecting at all.

"Hello, Dawn."

She opened her mouth but nothing came out.

"What's the matter, dear? Didn't Rick tell you I was coming?"

Her mother-in-law gave her a quick once over with her hard olive-green eyes then patted her dyed chestnut hair.

"Are you still in your dressing gown?"

"Yes actually, Fenella. I was having a nap. I've been told to rest."

"Yes, I know that." Fenella Beaumont sniffed. "So let's get you back to bed then."

She pushed her way into the house.

"My suitcase is in the car but Rick can get it when he comes home."

"Suitcase?"

"Yes, dear. I've come to stay."

Dawn's heart sank.

"Sorry?"

"It was going to be a surprise. Rick said not to let on."

I bet he did.

Dawn closed the door.

"Right, dear. It was a long drive so I'd love a cup of tea. I'll make it of course as you need to go back to bed."

'Of course. No. I mean… I'll make it now."

"I'll just go and powder my nose."

In the kitchen, Dawn filled the kettle and noticed that her hands were shaking. She couldn't believe that Fenella Beaumont was actually here. It wasn't that she didn't get on with her mother-in-law, more that she enjoyed the fact that they lived a good two hours' drive apart. It meant that family get-togethers were limited to once or twice a year. Fenella was a very proud and opinionated woman and Dawn always found being in her presence somewhat tiring. So the idea of dealing with Fenella in her current fragile condition was something that made her anxious.

It wasn't Rick's fault, of course. Dawn had never told him about the things his mother said that made her uneasy, or that led her to doubt her own abilities as a wife and mother. She'd never wanted him to be in a position where he felt awkward having the two women under the same roof. But then that had never happened on more than a handful of occasions and then it had only been for a night or two.

But now…

It seemed that Fenella Beaumont had come to stay and Dawn had no idea how long for. Or how she would manage. Or how this would help her to relax.

When she heard Rick's key turn in the lock, she took a deep breath. She had a feeling it was going to take all her strength to stay positive.

"I'm the winner!" James shouted as he ran into the hallway.

"Really James, I wasn't even racing you." Laura shook her head as she removed her coat, eight going on eighteen.

"Hello guys." Dawn opened her arms and hugged them both. "How was your day?"

"It was okay." Laura shrugged.

"Great, Mummy, we played football in afternoon playtime and I was the winner!"

"James!" Laura scowled at her brother.

"I was under the impression that footballers played in teams." Rick closed the door behind him.

"I told him that, Daddy, but he won't listen. He's just *obsessed* with winning."

"Good word, Laura." Dawn smiled.

"We had theassawsuses today for creative writing."

"Theassawsuses?" Dawn frowned.

"Yes, you know with all the different words in. Not to be confused with dictionaries!" She wagged a finger at her mother.

"Ah... you used a thesaurus."

"That's what I said, Mummy."

Dawn met Rick's laughing eyes and pulled a face. "Silly me. Uh, Rick... I think my other surprise has arrived."

"Oh?" He raised his eyebrows.

"Yes."

"Ohhhh... I thought I saw an unfamiliar car on the road. Dad no doubt changed it again." He shook his head. "Are you okay with the... uh... surprise?"

"What surprise, Daddy? I want to see!" James tugged at Rick's hand.

"Well if it isn't my beautiful grandchildren!"

"Nanna!"

"Nanna!"

Fenella enveloped the children in floral-scented bear hugs and Dawn suppressed a smile as she noticed James trying to wriggle free. He still liked hugs but didn't enjoy being squashed.

Then Fenella went to her son and took his face in her hands.

"Darling Rick, you look tired. Are you all right? I bet you're working too hard and trying to run the house now that Dawn's incapable. I mean incapacitated."

Rick glanced at Dawn, evidently uncomfortable with his mother's effusiveness and with her wording.

"Yes, I'm fine, thanks. It's Dawn that we've got to look out for."

"And that's why I'm here. To help you all out while darling Dawn rests."

Dawn swallowed her disappointment.

"Rick, be an angel and get my suitcase from the car. It's that flashy new Jag out on the road. Your father's choice, not mine. Laura and James, come with me and I'll fix you a healthy snack."

"There's food in the fridge actually," Dawn said. "Left over from lunchtime."

"Left over?" Fenella's drawn on eyebrows shot to her hairline.

"Yes. Allie brought lunch over for us... Rick asked her to. It was delicious. All freshly cooked and plenty of variety..."

Fenella shook her head. "Well, there'll be no need of that now I'm here. Nanna Beaumont will take care of everything, don't you worry."

But as her mother-in-law took Laura and James into the kitchen, Dawn was unable to comply. Of course she was worried. Fenella was overpowering, bossy and hard work at the best of times. Dawn needed to be at full-strength to deal with Fenella and right now she wasn't.

So she had a feeling that the duration of Fenella's stay would be challenging indeed.

The bedroom was grey with early morning light when Dawn woke. She blinked hard. It was too early to be awake yet something had disturbed her.

She held her breath and listened carefully, wondering if

it was one of the children. But neither of them was calling her.

Rick was on his side next to her, his breathing deep and regular.

So what was that banging?

She slid out of bed and shrugged into her dressing gown then crept across the landing and checked on Laura and James. They were both sleeping, Laura on her back with her hands on her chest like a fairy-tale princess, and James across his bed with his head hanging off the edge. She gently repositioned him so his head was on the pillow then tucked the duvet back around him.

As she pulled James's door closed behind her, she noticed that the door to the guest bedroom was open. She stuck her head around it and the bed was made, the curtains open and Fenella was nowhere to be seen. For a moment, she wondered if she'd imagined her mother-in-law's arrival, or if the older woman had decided to leave under cover of darkness like some blood-sucking vampire – only in Fenella's case it was soul-destroying she practised rather than drinking blood – but no, the dressing table was groaning under Fenella's paraphernalia. Bottles, jars, tubes, curlers, brushes, lipsticks and a small jewellery box had been arranged in order of size and colour.

Dawn shivered. From the look of that lot, Fenella was in for the long haul.

There was a book on the bedside table and Dawn peered at it, wondering what Fenella liked to read.

Walk With Poldark

She recalled Rick saying something about his mother's obsession with the TV show but apparently his father didn't feel the same. Married couples didn't have to like everything their partner liked, although she believed that they needed to have some common interests. Dawn and Rick did; they still laughed at the same things, still enjoyed spending time together. She just wished she could shake the final nagging worries about their relationship from her mind.

Downstairs, she steeled herself before entering the kitchen. The sounds coming from in there made her wonder what on earth was going on. There was the clattering of baking trays, the rustling of plastic and the grunting of a woman labouring. And not in childbirth. As she crept in, she almost screamed.

"Fenella... What have you done?"

"Sweet peas and piglets, Dawn! You frightened me half to death."

"I... I'm sorry but what..." Dawn stared at the kitchen she had loved the moment she'd seen it, with its clean cream-shaker cupboard doors and its black-granite worktops. She'd had everything where she wanted it; from the free-standing range cooker to the coffee machine and the digital radio Rick had bought her last Christmas that resembled an old jukebox.

But now...

Everything had been moved and the surfaces that she made an effort to keep scratch-free, were covered in things that Fenella had pulled from her cupboards, the things Dawn kept even though she knew she'd never use them. She fought the urge to check under the cast-iron bake stone that had been moved from the top of the range – where she kept it for making pancakes and Welsh cakes – and dumped onto the worktop next to the sink. It was very heavy and could easily scratch the granite if not handled carefully. She wondered if her mother-in-law had considered this.

"I've been giving everything a good clean and sort for you."

"But I didn't ask you to."

Fenella held up a hand. "I know you didn't, dear, but let's be honest, it needed it. And had done for quite some time. Once I've finished cleaning out the cupboards, you can help me to decide what's going out."

"Going out?"

"Yes of course. There's a lot of junk here."

"But…" Dawn bit her lip. There was no point keeping on with the *buts*. Fenella was obviously trying to help and she didn't mean any harm. "Okay."

"Why don't you have a cup of tea first though?"

"Yes. I think I will. Do you want one?"

"Not for me. I'd rather keep going."

Dawn made tea for her and Rick, trying not to stare at Fenella as she continued her mission. Because that's clearly what it was. She intended to sort out the kitchen and would not be stopped.

"I'm going to take this up to Rick." Dawn held up two mugs.

"You do that. I'll call you in about an hour, shall I?"

Dawn glanced at the clock on the wall.

"It's only five-thirty."

"Early bird catches the germ."

"Worm."

Fenella threw back her head and laughed. "In this case, it's the germ, dear. The germs in this kitchen must have been having the party of a lifetime."

"Right," Dawn forced out the word through gritted teeth. "No need to call me. I'll be up soon enough."

She left the kitchen quickly before Fenella could deliver any further insults, then climbed the stairs, taking care not to spill the tea. After all, she didn't want to give the older woman something else to comment on.

"I'm sure she didn't mean it like that. She was just joking, Dawnie."

Rick smiled at her. As she took in his sleep-rumpled hair and his broad shoulders, currently bare due to the fact that he only ever wore a t-shirt in bed when it was freezing out, she tried not to be distracted. She knew how yummy his warm skin would smell if she snuggled into him and how good it would be to have his strong arms wrapped around her.

"I don't think she was, Rick. She basically told me that I'm a slob."

"You're not a slob."

"Your mother thinks I am."

He shook his head.

"Anyway, how long's she staying?"

"I told you last night, as long as you need her."

But I don't need her.

Dawn took a swig of tea to prevent the response escaping. The last thing she wanted to do was appear ungrateful and upset her husband. He was just trying to help and she knew he'd feel terrible going back to work if he thought she'd be struggling and risking her health and the baby.

"Rick, I need some sort of idea how long because I like some space. You know... when I'm at home."

"Dawnie," he took her hand and kissed it, "I need to know you'll be okay when I'm not here. I'll worry anyway but at least if Mum is with you, you'll have to take it easy."

"But she'll change the whole house around."

Rick kissed the tip of each of her fingers and Dawn's mind grew fuzzy.

"No she won't. I'll have a gentle word with her."

He ran soft kisses along her wrist and Dawn struggled to focus on her point.

"And... ask her not to throw anything out without checking first?"

Rick let go of her hand then kissed her cheek before picking up his tea.

"Of course."

Dawn sank back onto the pillows.

"Now how about we grab another hour of snuggling before the children wake up? You know I love any excuse to feel your curvy body against mine." He wiggled his eyebrows.

"I thought you said we shouldn't—"

"Well yes... but I can still show you how much I love you, can't I?"

He opened his arms and Dawn moved into them, the warmth of his body and his delicious male scent making her love him even more.

Then Rick's mouth met hers and she floated away, caught on a cloud of love and desire, until their bedroom door swung open and heavy footsteps entered the room.

"Rick, dear?"

He poked his head above the covers.

"Mum?"

"I need your help moving something downstairs."

He rubbed his eyes as Dawn peered out from beneath the quilt too.

"Can't it wait, Fenella?"

"I'm afraid not, Dawn."

"All right, Mum, I'll be down in a minute."

"Don't be long!"

Fenella left with a humph and Rick slumped against the pillows.

"She can't go bursting in like that, Rick."

He met her eyes and she saw uncertainty wavering in his. "No, I know. I guess she's just finding her feet around here."

"Finding her feet?"

"I'll have a word."

"Please do. And quickly. Because I can't deal with this if we're not going to have any privacy, Rick."

He nodded.

"I'll get dressed and go and see what she wants."

Dawn turned onto her side and closed her eyes. She kept them closed until she heard him leave the bedroom, because she didn't want him to see her tears. The last thing she wanted was for Rick to feel torn between his wife and mother; that wouldn't be fair at all. But she hoped he really would ask Fenella to tone it down a bit, or having her around would cause more damage than it would if Dawn was left alone to manage. And with her marriage already being a bit unsteady – at least in her own head – Dawn didn't think she had the energy to deal with an interfering mother-in-law too.

9

"This chocolate cake is delicious, Allie," Camilla said before she took another bite.

"It really is." Honey smacked her lips. "You're going to make us fat."

"Some of us already are." Dawn rubbed her belly.

"That's not fat, you're just keeping my niece or nephew warm." Camilla smiled at Dawn across the table.

"Thanks, Camilla."

"What are big sisters for?"

"How are things going with the mother-in-law, Dawn?" Allie asked.

"Monster-in-law more like," Camilla blurted.

"Camilla!" Dawn frowned at her sister.

The women had gathered for a Tuesday evening get-together at The Cosy Cottage Café. It had become their routine and only didn't happen if someone was ill, away, or if there was, in Dawn's case, a childcare issue. Dawn hadn't been able to make the previous Tuesday because of her condition but this week, as she was feeling stronger, she'd wanted to come. To get out of the house for a bit while she could.

"I'll be honest with you... my house has never been so clean."

"Well that's fabulous. Wish someone would come and clean mine," Allie joked. "But that's not a good thing for you because..."

"I don't want to seem ungrateful."

"You can tell us anything," Camilla said.

"I'm not so sure about that. I mean, you just called her my monster-in-law and I only ever said that once when I was drunk. And I didn't mean it. Fenella tries hard, it's just that she's also—"

"Very trying?" Honey finished her sentence, her brown eyes warm and understanding.

"Yes." Dawn put her fork down. "She's cleaned everything from cupboards to shoes to behind the downstairs toilet, but it's strange having another woman doing that. It's like my space has been invaded."

"A space-invader monster-in-law!" Camilla snorted. "Well Rick should have been doing his fair share too, Dawnie." She took a swig of her wine.

"I've told you before that he does what he can but with his job and the hours he works, it's very difficult. That's why we have had more traditional roles, I guess."

"It was like that with Roger and me," Allie said.

"Was it?"

"He was..."

"Difficult. A chauvinist." Camilla took Allie's hand. "You don't have to be kind about him in front of us, you know."

"I know. I just don't like calling him over. It seems like I'm betraying the kids."

Dawn and the other women knew how tough life had

been for Allie in the past. She'd revealed some of the details of her marriage to them that summer, after Chris Monroe had arrived in town, and they'd been shocked that she'd kept them to herself for so long. But Dawn knew that people did keep secrets, even from their friends and relatives. She'd been glad that Allie had unburdened herself and it was wonderful to see her so happy with Chris now.

"Rick isn't a chauvinist though, Camilla."

"I know that. He just needs a bit of a kick up the bum sometimes to get him into gear."

"He'd do more if he had more time."

Camilla nodded. "All right, all right. I know how much you love him."

"And as for Fenella, as much as she might be... treading on my toes, she's the one looking after Laura and James this evening."

"It'll be good for her to spend some time with them." Allie smiled. "It's nice for children to have extended family."

"James isn't so sure. He was delighted at first but now he knows that she's going to make him eat his greens and tidy up the toy room when he's finished playing, he's not so sure. And she's making Laura practise her times tables every night, which my daughter does not find amusing."

Dawn thought of the rhythmic chanting that took place after the children had eaten dinner. Still, it was how she'd learned her tables and every child should know them.

"I can understand how it must be challenging but try to take whatever time you can to rest, Dawn. You need it. I doubt she'll stay permanently?" Allie ended on a question.

"God I hope not. Can you imagine?"

"She'd be getting you to express so she could test the quality of your milk." Camilla giggled. "Sorry! I think I've had too much wine. Just let her know if she's bugging you."

Dawn nodded but inside she was wilting. Fenella had been with them for just five days and her domineering presence had left Dawn drained. Keeping her mouth shut when her mother-in-law made sniping remarks was taking all the strength she had. But she didn't want to snap and hurt the older woman and she also didn't want to seem ungrateful.

"I'm sure she'll leave in a week or so."

"Doesn't her husband want her at home then?" Honey asked, twirling a strand of her rainbow-dyed hair around her fingers. "You'd think he'd have come too."

"He's probably enjoying all the extra time he can spend on his boat, playing chess, golfing and whatever else it is that he does now."

Dawn thought of her father-in-law and how he liked his time outdoors, often spending weekends at the docks or out on the water. When he wasn't sailing the boat, he was polishing it or conducting repairs. At least that's what he told Fenella and she seemed to have bought into it. Was that what happened to marriages long-term then, if they went the distance? Did people accept their partner's excuses because it was easier to nod along, or because they just liked having time apart?

Something struck her then.

What if Fenella was actually lonely?

After all, Rick's younger brother, Kyle, had moved away straight after university, just like Rick had. Kyle had a family of his own now and he lived on the Isle of Wight with his wife and three-year-old twin girls. So it was possible that Fenella didn't see much of him, although she never let on.

Dawn was overwhelmed by a wave of compassion for Rick's mother. It couldn't be easy when your children left, especially if they moved far away.

She resolved to try to be extra kind to Fenella when she

went home later, and to try to make her mother-in-law feel appreciated. Because everyone deserved that, didn't they?

"Hello?"

Dawn locked the front door behind her.

"Fenella?"

"SHHH!" Came from the top of the stairs followed by the appearance of her mother-in-law in a long white nightgown with a frilly collar, that made Dawn think of those she'd seen in faded Victorian photographs.

"Hi Fenella. Where are the children?"

"In bed, of course." Fenella replied as she descended the stairs, shrugging into a purple cord dressing gown. "I've read them both a story and they're fast asleep."

Dawn checked the clock on the wall. "But it's only eight. Are you sure they're sleeping?"

"I did have children of my own you know." Fenella scowled at her.

"Oh, I know that. It's just that even when James drops off, Laura often takes a while. She tends to spend time thinking and processing her day before she goes to sleep. A few times I've even found her still awake when I've popped up to check on her and it's after nine."

"After nine?" Fenella tutted. "No wonder that little girl has trouble concentrating."

"What do you mean?"

Dawn removed her coat and hung it over the bannister. Fenella eyed it then gave a small shake of her head.

"She told me she's having trouble with maths."

"When?"

"Yesterday. I didn't want to worry you."

"Well you should have told me. When I saw her teacher recently, she didn't say there was a problem."

"Hmmmm. Well if she got more sleep there wouldn't be."

"Fenella..." Dawn took a deep breath.

"Yes."

"Oh... nothing. I'll just pop up to give them a kiss then make us a cup of tea. Rick's not back yet then?"

"No. He's rather late too, isn't he?"

"He's been later. It depends what time he gets out of work. I'll text him to find out when he'll be back."

Fenella nodded then went into the kitchen and Dawn climbed the stairs. She'd had a lovely evening at the café and coming home to Fenella's disapproval was difficult, especially as she just wanted to put her pyjamas on and lie on the sofa watching some mindless TV. And she'd been intending on being kind to her mother-in-law.

Upstairs, she pushed James's door open and found him sleeping across the bed, so she gently wriggled him around, then kissed his forehead. He smelt of honey and lemon and a scent that was all his own, one that she'd know in a room full of children even if she was blindfolded. He was her little boy and her heart brimmed over with love for him.

When she went into Laura's room, she crossed the pink rug to the bed and leaned over. Laura turned suddenly and sat up.

"I thought you'd still be awake."

"Oh Mummy, you know I need to read before I go to sleep. But Nanny said I couldn't. I told her she was being a big fat bossy boots."

Dawn swallowed a giggle. "You didn't?"

Dawn saw a look of scorn passed over Laura's face in the light from the hallway.

"Well I almost did. I said she was a bossy boots but I didn't say the fat bit. Mummy... when's she going home? I like her and everything but she's not like you. She has different rules and ways of doing things and I don't like them. I want it to be just the four of us again."

Dawn brushed Laura's hair from her cheek then sighed. "I know, angel, that's how I like it too. Nanna's just here to help for a few weeks until I feel better."

"But you are all better aren't you? And the baby is okay now."

"Yes, I do feel much better. But it would be mean if we just told Nanna that and sent her packing."

"Sent her packing?"

"Yes... on her way, back home."

"Oh. Yes. Well let her stay a bit longer, but then send her packing."

Dawn smiled. "Deal. But try to be nice and polite for now."

"Mummy, can I read now, please?"

Dawn chewed her lip. If she said yes, she'd be going against what Fenella had told Laura to do but if she said no, Laura could well be awake when she came up to bed.

"For fifteen minutes. But no longer. Promise?"

"Pinky promise." Laura nodded then switched on the lamp that was on her bedside table.

"And it's our secret."

"Of course, Mummy. Between you and me." Laura tapped the side of her nose.

Dawn was still smiling when she reached the kitchen. Laura was so much like Rick with his mannerisms and vocabulary, yet also so much like her. Dawn remembered struggling to sleep in her youth and lying in bed with her mind racing about everything from politics to whether or not Take That would ever get back together.

"Something funny, Dawn? Do share, I could do with a laugh." Fenella was sat at the breakfast bar with a steaming mug of tea.

"Oh, I was just thinking about how much I love the children."

"They are lovely. And even if I do think they stay up too late, you and Rick have done a good job, I must admit."

"Uh... thank you." Here she went again, being such a contradictory and confusing character. One minute, Fenella was undermining her, the next she was building her up. Albeit as a veiled compliment.

"Did you text Rick?"

"I forgot. I'll do it now."

Dawn dug her mobile out of her trouser pocket and swiped the screen. It buzzed as a message popped up.

Staying in London tonight, Dawn. Late one working through, so no point coming home. Ring you in the morning. Rick X

What?

Blood whooshed through her ears and her head spun. He was staying out all night. Granted, he'd done it before when he had an important meeting or a very early start but never at this short notice. Now she'd be left on her own with Fenella and she didn't know where he was sleeping. Or who he was with.

"I've uh... I've got to do something a moment. I'll be back shortly," she said to her mother-in-law.

"But Dawn…"

She opened the back door and went into the garden before Fenella could argue. This just wasn't on. What did Rick think he was playing at? She brought up her contacts list and scrolled down to *Rick* then pressed the call button.

When he answers, he's going to get a mouthful.

As she listened to the phone ringing, her breaths came shaky and fast.

No, not a mouthful but a few strong words.

It kept on ringing.

Okay then, some questions.

Perhaps but…

His voice came on at the other end and she was about to say his name then realised she'd got his voicemail.

She waited until the recorded message finished then was besieged by doubts so she ended the call.

Should she leave him a message?

Yes, of course.

She dialled him again and waited for voicemail to kick in.

"Hi Rick, it's me… Dawn… you know, your wife. Hope you're okay. Could you ring me. Even if it's late when you get this. I just want to hear your voice. Love you."

She stared at the black screen, seeing her face reflected there: pale, large eyes wide, fear in her gaze.

"What did he say?" Fenella was peering out of the door.

"He's not answering. But I left a message."

"Cup of tea in here for you."

"Thanks."

As she followed Fenella inside, the last thing Dawn wanted to do was to sit and drink tea, but if she didn't, she knew she'd go upstairs and cry. Although what comfort she'd get from the older woman, she didn't know. But at least it would be distracting and hopefully stop her imagining that Rick might be out drinking with women, smart attractive women in tight dresses and high heels, the type who worked hard and partied hard, who lived without commitments. Women who were a bit like Camilla.

Women who might not mind if a man had a wife in a little country village because they didn't want any commitment anyway.

She shook her head as if to shake the disturbing thoughts away, still holding her mobile tightly as she willed Rick to call. Just to put her mind at rest. If that were at all possible.

"So who is he staying with?" Fenella asked as she poured fresh tea from a teapot that Dawn didn't recognise.

"I'm not sure."

"You don't know?" Fenella frowned. "Well I wouldn't have that."

"Look, I can hardly order him around can I? Besides, he didn't answer so I'm helpless right now."

The reality of the situation swept over her. "I can't even have a stiff drink to try to calm my churning belly or to at least numb my nerves. I want to know where he is tonight. But I don't have any idea…"

She glanced at Fenella and found that the older woman's eyes were wide as she stared at her. Great. So now she seemed like a suspicious neurotic wife.

"Of course you do. I'm sorry, Dawn, that was unfair of me. You must be worried."

Again, Dawn had to try to keep the surprise off her face. "I am."

Fenella pushed a mug of tea across the breakfast bar. "Drink this. It might help with your upset stomach."

"Thank you."

"You know... I'm quite annoyed at Rick."

"You are?"

"He shouldn't do this to you. I mean, you've just had a pregnancy scare. That's why I'm here after all, and he's decided to stay in London without warning you before hand."

Dawn sipped her tea. She was a boiling pot of contradiction right now, torn between being angry at Rick herself and wanting to defend him from his own mother. And that was ridiculous as Fenella was actually being supportive.

"Why don't you try to get some sleep and I'll stay up for a bit. Just in case he rings."

"But he'll probably ring my mobile if he does call."

"Well you can leave that with me if you like so it doesn't disturb you... or take it upstairs..." Fenella smiled. "Because you probably won't rest at all if it's not right beside you."

Dawn nodded.

"I guess I should try to get some rest."

"You certainly should. Now take your tea up and get into bed. Perhaps have a read."

"Thanks, I will."

"Dawn?"

"Yes?"

"I am only here to help, you know. I'm sorry if I sometimes seem overbearing."

"You're not overbearing, Fenella."

"Really?"

"Well... uh..."

Fenella nodded. "I know I can be. I just... when Rick

called me, I was extremely worried about you and the baby but I was also grateful."

"Grateful?"

"To feel needed. That's why I wanted to help as much as I could and cleaning was one way I hoped to make myself useful. But afterwards, I realised that perhaps it was a bit out of order. After all, this is your home and there I was sticking my nose in. Paul did warn me before I left. He told me not to try to take over, as I can be quite overpowering when I do. He said I'd soon get my marching orders if I stuck my nose in too far and look at me... I've been doing exactly that."

"No, Fenella, I'm really grateful. Honestly."

"Thank you, Dawn. You're too kind." She sighed. "You know... oh it doesn't matter."

"No it does. Please go on."

"Are you sure? I don't really have anyone to talk to about these things and sometimes, it all builds up."

"You can tell me, Fenella."

"Thank you, dear. When Paul retired, I thought we were going to do all the things we'd planned years ago. We have National Trust membership and I was looking forward to visiting the places we'd admired for so long. He used to show me all these beautiful stately homes and castles on Instagram and we'd talk about how we'd visit them."

"And it hasn't happened?"

She shook her head. "He's always still so busy and I don't like to ask."

"But you should, Fenella. You have a right to spend time with him too."

"It's like retiring gave him a new lease of life and it doesn't involve me. I can't play golf, I'm terrified of going out on that damned boat because I can't swim very well and I'm not that good on social media, so I can't even get involved with Wallace and Lulu's Instagram page."

"You could learn how to do that. If you like, I'll show you."

"I'd be very grateful for some lessons in that respect, Dawn."

"No problem at all. But what will you do about Paul? You should be honest with him because perhaps he doesn't even realise that he's neglecting you."

Fenella shrugged. "Perhaps I will. Or I'll just get on with it, I guess. I'm good at that. My sons and their families don't live close enough to visit every week, and Dawn, please don't think that's a criticism. My husband prefers sailing and golf to taking me around stately homes and castles. All I do have to enjoy is a slightly wicked crush on a TV character."

Dawn smiled.

"You know, Fenella... It would really help us out if you could come to stay more regularly. Perhaps you could pick the children up from school once a week – I could speak to the head teacher and get your name on the trusted contacts list – and you could help me out with the baby. Even once a fortnight if it's too far to drive on a weekly basis."

Fenella nodded. "That's very kind, Dawn. I promise that I won't do any cleaning unless you ask me to do it."

"That's settled then."

"Every other Thursday?"

"Whatever suits you."

"Now go and get some rest, dear."

"Thank you. Good night, Fenella."

"Call if you need me."

Upstairs, Dawn changed into her fluffy pyjamas then slipped under the quilt. A noise outside made her jump but she realised it was the wind. It had been breezy all day and the wind was now picking up. Perhaps the weather was changing and the Indian summer they'd talked about was on its way out.

She wondered what Rick was doing. Was he sleeping or engaged in conversation in some swanky London club? Was he poring over figures and offering advice, or was he laughing with some attractive woman who was pawing at his arm and fingering his tie as she hung on his every word...

Stop it!

This wouldn't do anyone any good.

She picked up the top book off the pile on her bedside table – a psychological thriller that had been raved about recently – and opened it. But the words swam before her eyes and she tried to read the page four times before realising that this wasn't going to work. Instead, she tried to think about her conversation with Fenella. It had been one of revelations and she hoped that their relationship would be stronger because of it. And that Fenella would feel needed, because she hated to think of anyone feeling lonely or left out. There was no need for that at all.

10

Dawn woke to a buzzing sound. She reached for her mobile then peered at the screen. It was six o'clock and she'd received an alert from the mobile network about cinema tickets. As if that would be her first concern on waking. She realised that she must have fallen asleep trying to meditate, as the lamp on her bedside table was still on. Exhaustion had obviously claimed her in spite of her reservations about being able to rest.

She sat up and propped the pillows up behind her then took a few deep breaths before looking at her mobile again. There were no missed calls and no text messages. Rick hadn't tried to make contact at all.

Well she was not going to spend the day moping around. There was probably a perfectly good reason why her husband had not called her and she would have to give him the benefit of the doubt or go mad. Besides, all this stress wouldn't be good for the baby.

She got up, showered, dressed then went downstairs. Fenella was in the kitchen making pancakes. Laura and

James were sitting at the breakfast bar, fully dressed, tucking into pancakes covered in chopped banana.

"Good morning," Dawn said as she kissed their heads.

"Morning, Mummy."

"Hi, Mummy."

"Morning, Dawn. Pancakes?"

"Uh... yes, please. I actually feel quite peckish."

Fenella handed her a plate then loaded it with two pancakes and gestured at the bottle of maple syrup. "You want that, bananas or both?"

"Banana will be fine, thanks."

Fenella nodded then chopped up a banana into a bowl and passed it to Dawn.

"Thank you." Dawn smiled at her mother-in-law and saw warmth in the older woman's eyes. It lifted her own spirits and she wondered if it was usually there, and if she failed to see it because she had a version of Fenella in her head and that version hadn't been warm and kind. Until now.

"I was thinking that I can drop the children off at school this morning then go shopping for you. Do you want to write a list?"

Dawn swallowed the banana she'd been chewing.

"That's really kind of you, thank you."

"I'll do that then when I come back, I'll pack my things."

"What?"

"Well it's probably time for me to be going, Dawn. Give you some space to sort things out here."

"You don't have to do that."

Fenella nodded. "I do. You're better now and if you need me again, you just ring and I'll come straight back. But you and your family need some time alone to prepare for the little one."

"But who will make me pancakes, Nanna?" James asked.

"I'll make extra then freeze them, so all your mum needs to do is heat them up in the mornings. How does that sound?"

"Like a good plan."

Dawn smiled at her son. He was so easily bought with food.

"Nanna is going to visit more often now, so she'll be able to make you pancakes when she comes."

"Are you, Nanna?"

Fenella nodded. "Whenever your mummy needs me."

Laura was chewing absently, silently, her eyes focused on something in the garden.

"Laura, what's up?"

"Nothing."

"Are you sure?"

"I just need to check on Lulu and Wallace before school, so I'm trying to eat my breakfast quickly."

"Good idea."

When they'd finished eating, the children went outside and Dawn helped Fenella to tidy the kitchen.

"Thank you."

"What for?"

"Well, for being understanding."

"I might seem like a pompous old bag at times but I do mean well, you know." Fenella shook the cloth she'd used to wipe the cooker top over the sink then rinsed it.

"You're not a pompous old bag."

Fenella chuckled.

"We all go through trials in life, Dawn, and marriage certainly isn't easy. I do hope that you and Rick manage to sort this out but even if you don't, I hope you'll be happy. Life is so short."

She placed a hand on Dawn's shoulder. "You're a good mum and a loving wife. You deserve to be treated well. Make sure you're honest with Rick. Do not let him off the hook."

Dawn inclined her head.

"Same goes for you with Paul."

"Unfortunately, I'm not very good at practising what I preach." Fenella pressed her lips together.

"Mummy!

James ran into the kitchen.

"No, I want to say!" Laura pushed past him and stood in front of Dawn panting.

"What is it?" Dawn scanned her children's red faces, met their shining eyes.

"It's Wallace."

Oh no... not again... The new one couldn't possibly have died too.

"What's wrong with Wallace?" Dawn steeled herself.

"Come and see!" James grabbed her hand and pulled her outside.

In the garden, Laura knelt in front of the hutch then slowly opened the door to the sleeping compartment. Dawn noticed that her daughter had put Lulu into the garden run. She steeled herself, preparing to see a stiff little body, but instead, Wallace was there, eyes wide and nose twitching as he spotted his owners.

"Wallace is a mummy!" James shouted.

Dawn stared in shock at the straw.

From behind her, Fenella laughed. "How on earth did that happen? Wallace is a boy isn't he? And even if he wasn't... You only have one guinea pig don't you?"

"Yes." Dawn turned to meet her mother-in-law's eyes then she winked at her. "I'll explain later."

"Yay! Can we keep them all?"

Dawn looked at the four tiny white guinea pigs, then at her children's delighted expressions and knew that she couldn't refuse. They'd already lost one guinea pig, even if they knew nothing about it, so she could hardly deny them this.

"I guess so. But I think we'd better give them some darkness now and close the door so they don't get cold. Wallace has a big job ahead of him... I mean her."

"Wallace is a girl!" Laura shrieked then she held her belly as she giggled.

"Indeed she is."

"Can we have a boy baby then Mummy, because there are too many girls now." James frowned, his light brown brows meeting in the middle of his smooth forehead.

"I'll see what I can do." Dawn ruffled his hair then ushered the children towards the house. "Come on, time to get ready for school."

Fenella led them inside and Dawn turned and gazed at the garden. Lulu was hopping about in the run, stopping to nibble at the grass. Dawn realised that it was lucky that the rabbit hadn't attacked the baby guinea pigs – she thought she recalled reading that they were called pups – or even eaten them. That thought turned her stomach but she knew she'd read about rabbits turning on their own young. They would need to get another hutch now to give Wallace some space to raise her family. Especially as it had turned colder and Lulu couldn't stay out in the run all day.

More than ever, she wished her husband was here, so she could speak to him about what had happened and so that he could help her to decide on what needed to be done.

She stepped inside the kitchen and closed the door.

Then her heart leapt as she spotted Rick standing in the hallway, his face dark with stubble, his eyes red and his suit crumpled as if he'd slept in it. Laura and James were clinging to his hands, asking him why he'd come home from work at this time and Fenella was trying to get them to go upstairs to brush their teeth.

"Laura, James, go on upstairs. I'll be up in a bit." Dawn used her strictest voice and the children listened, as if aware that their parents needed some time alone.

"I'll be upstairs if you need me." Fenella gave a quick wave.

Then it was just Dawn and her husband and the air was filled with tension so thick she could barely breathe.

"I am so sorry," he whispered. "I've done something terrible."

Dawn wobbled and Rick was suddenly beside her, taking her arm. He helped her to a chair and she sat down then placed her palms flat on the kitchen table as if to anchor herself.

Rick took the chair next to hers and sat facing her. She noticed that he couldn't keep his hands still, he was wringing them together, his knuckles were white and his cuticles were ragged as if he'd been chewing them through the night.

"So you've done something terrible?"

"Yes. Well I think so. Although it might not be terrible… it depends how you see it, really."

"Something unforgiveable?"

"I'm not sure."

The ground shifted beneath her and she gasped.

"Dawn?"

"I'm all right. Just a bit dizzy."

"I am so sorry for putting you through all of this."

"Rick, if you'd just let me know where you were last night. I was so worried."

"God, I know." He rubbed his eyes with the heels of his hands. "I'm sorry, I was in such a state. Jake took me to a bar and we got drunk and... I'm just sorry. I was in no fit state to come home."

"You didn't come home because you got drunk? What if something had been wrong with one of the children or with the baby... I wouldn't have been able to reach you."

Dawn expected to feel anger rising again but instead a strange numbness was taking over, spreading like ice through her limbs and dulling her thoughts. Making them sluggish.

"Dawn, I'd better just get straight to the point here. I got drunk because of what I did."

"Did you... did you cheat, Rick?"

She clamped her jaw shut to stop herself crying, although a lump had risen in her throat and her eyes were burning.

"Did I cheat?" His bloodshot eyes widened. "Me?"

"You've been acting strangely. You've been distant. You didn't come home last night and now you're telling me you did something terrible. What's worse than cheating?"

"Dawnie, I love you, I would never cheat on you. Is that what you thought?"

"Well look at me!" She gestured at her jogging bottoms and baggy t-shirt then at her face, where she knew she had a line from a crease in the pillowcase. Her hair was pulled into a messy ponytail and she certainly didn't feel at her most attractive.

"Look at you? Dawn you're the most beautiful woman I've ever seen."

"But right now I'm all fat and swollen and…" Her lip wobbled so she stopped talking.

"You're absolutely gorgeous. I love you so much and even if you put on twenty stone, I'd still love you because you would be you. Don't you get that? And right now, your body is changing again because you're carrying our baby. That, to me, makes you even more beautiful."

"Really?"

He took her hands. "Really. I'll never ever want anyone else. That's why I married you. I have never ever cheated and I never ever will."

"So what's wrong then? Why all the secretive phone calls and longer hours and the distance between us? When you were home last week, things seemed so much better but then you stay out all night…"

"If you think I've been distant then I'm sorry. I didn't mean to be at all. I've just had a lot on my mind. I did before you found out you were pregnant again but it kind of added to the pressure."

"It wasn't the best time, was it?"

He shook his head. "No, but I don't care about the timing now. I'm delighted that we'll have another child, but for me, I need to be able to provide for you all. I want you to be happy and secure and if you've been feeling the opposite of that then it's an ironic mess."

"Oh Rick." She squeezed his hands.

"Dawn… yesterday I quit my job."

"What?"

"I quit. Well, I didn't exactly walk out empty-handed but the company has suffered some losses recently and they asked for volunteers to come forward to accept redundancies."

Dawn's mouth had fallen open so she forced it shut.

"You don't need to worry, Dawnie, it's a good package. I wouldn't have considered it otherwise. I promise you that."

"You gave up your job?'

His cheeks blanched. "You're not happy. See, this is why I was concerned you'd think it was terrible. The last thing I want to do is to put you under more pressure. But honestly, angel, we have more than enough money to pay the mortgage and bills for two years... more if we're careful. I know it's not the best time to be careful with money with a new baby on the way but I won't just sit around doing nothing. I have some ideas... and contacts. I know people who'd give me a job tomorrow. I'll need to go into the City for a few days next week just to tie up loose ends but then I'll be free."

Dawn started to laugh.

"Dawnie?"

"Rick, I'm not worried. We still have money that we saved when I was working. We won't be broke; I know that. And if it came to it we could sell this house and downsize."

"I don't want to do that to you and the children."

"No, I know. But it's always an option. And after the baby's born, I could look for work. Do some supply teaching just to keep some money coming in. I was hoping to go back to work anyway, wasn't I... before we found out we were expecting again?"

"So you're not mad?"

"Not at all. In fact, I'm delighted. Just think of the time we can spend together. It was so lovely having you home last week."

"Well, that was one of my ideas. I could set up as an independent financial adviser. Work mainly from home and go out when necessary. It would mean I'd be around more for when baby number three comes."

"Oh Rick I love that idea."

"And if you want to return to work next year, then that's up to you, but you know you don't need to."

"I know that, but I think I'd like to. Even if it's just for a day or two a week."

Her heart soared as she let everything sink in. Rick wouldn't be working such long hours anymore. He wouldn't have to leave for the train at the crack of dawn or return after Laura and James had gone to bed. It would be so good for the children. So good for them.

Then a thought struck her like a bucket of ice-cold water.

The email.

There was still the issue of the email.

"Rick."

"Yes."

"There's one more thing."

He nodded.

"I was upset... because I'd got it into my head that you were cheating. And I'm so glad that isn't the case but I did something I shouldn't have."

"You did?" He watched her, his hazel eyes wary.

"I went into your email account."

He shrugged. "I wouldn't have thought you'd do that but there's nothing in there to worry about."

"I found an email. Titled FYEO. About a weekend away. From another woman. Brianna Mandrell."

Understanding filled his eyes.

"Ahhhhh..."

"But you're not cheating?"

He smiled. "No, but I'm gutted you found that. It was meant to be a surprise. I was trying to organise a weekend away for us without the children. I'd enlisted Camilla and your mother to take care of Laura and James. I wanted to take you away for a weekend of pampering, to ensure that you got some rest and so that we could have some quality time together."

"It was about a booking for us?"

"Of course."

Relief washed over her.

"Rick, I'm so relieved. I spoke to Camilla and she insisted it was nothing to worry about and said she'd speak to you. It all makes sense now. She was probably going to tell you to talk to me about it, so I'd stop worrying."

He opened his arms and she moved into them, sitting on his lap as he kissed her gently.

"I thought I was losing you."

"You'll never lose me."

"I love you."

"And I love you."

"Daddy!" James shot into the kitchen closely pursued by a red-faced Fenella.

"James! Come here right now. I'm so sorry. I told him you needed time to talk but he was desperate to tell you." Fenella straightened her blouse.

"Daddy!"

"No let me tell him." Laura ran up to her father and took hold of his face. "Stop looking at Mummy for a minute and concentrate."

Rick winked at Dawn then nodded at his daughter.

"Laura, you have my undivided attention."

"Good."

"It's Wallace," James blurted. "He's a girl."

"James!" Laura turned to her brother. "Shut up."

"Wallace is a girl?" Rick's eyebrows shot up and colour flooded his cheeks then he started laughing. "Well that's a shocker. But how do you know for sure?"

Laura folded her arms and rolled her eyes. "She had babies Daddy."

"Babies?"

"Yes. Lots of tiny white babies and Mummy said we're going to keep them all." James jumped up and down. "Yay for baby guinea pigs!"

"Let's go and see them again, James."

The children hurried out into the garden.

"I take it that you two worked things out then?" Fenella eyed them both. "Not my business, I know... well it is because I love you both and want you and my grandchildren to be happy... and you look... happier."

"Everything's sorted, Fenella. Life is going to be much better now for all of us."

"I'll fill you in later, Mum," Rick said. "But right now I think we'd better go and check that James isn't handling the new additions to the family. He'll scare them half to death."

"And we don't want another dead guinea pig round here." Dawn gasped as she realised what she'd just said.

Fenella frowned. "Another dead guinea pig?"

"Something else I'll explain," Rick said.

They followed Fenella out into the garden and Dawn's heart was so full of love that she thought she might just float off into the sky, if Rick wasn't holding her hand so tight.

11

"Oooh, look Mummy!" James pointed at The Cosy Cottage Café as they walked through the gate. The path and steps were lined with pumpkins of varying sizes. Each one had a different expression and glowed in the twilight. Dawn knew they had LED tealights inside them instead of naked flames. Allie always considered the safest option with children around, which Dawn was glad of as James's curiosity meant he'd probably try to examine their light source.

The trees in the café garden and the pergola were draped with strings of tiny pumpkin-shaped lights and a few black bats dangled from them, swaying in the gentle evening breeze.

The front of the café itself was dressed with fake cobwebs that hung from the shutters, and to the side of the front door, was a four-foot skeleton. As the café door opened and Allie emerged carrying a tray, the skeleton cackled and shook.

"Mummy, it's alive!" James grabbed her hand.

"Don't be silly, James," Laura said. "It's obviously activated when someone goes near it, which means it has a movement sensor."

Dawn looked at Rick and he shrugged. "I guess she's learned about it in school."

"Or watching the Discovery Channel."

"Hello!" Allie called as she approached them, depositing the tray she was carrying on a nearby table.

In keeping with the café theme, Allie was dressed as a giant pumpkin. She was wearing black tights and boots with a velvet pumpkin dress that hung to her knees. On her head was a green headband with a thick green stalk sticking out of it. She'd tied her hair back and painted her face orange.

"You look amazing, Allie. You always make such an effort."

Allie smiled warmly.

"Have you seen Jordan and Max yet?"

Dawn looked around and spotted the young men at the drinks table. She took in their matching grey werewolf costumes. They'd outlined their eyes with coal pencil and drawn whiskers around their stick on snouts.

"I told them they'd terrify the children looking like that but Jordan insisted that kids these days aren't scared by werewolves. Popular culture means that if they saw a zombie walking along the street they wouldn't bat an eyelid." Allie shook her head.

"How things change, eh?"

"And you guys look great! Laura, I think you are the scariest vampire I've ever seen."

"I'm not a vampire, I'm a witch."

"Oh!" Allie grimaced at Dawn. "Of course you are. And James... you are a terrifying ghost."

"You can see me?"

"Who said that?" Allie frowned and batted the air around her, causing James to giggle.

"You can see me when I say you can," James said, throwing back the hood of the white robe that Dawn had fashioned out of an old sheet. It was a simple costume but James had insisted that he wanted to be a ghost like the ones in the old movies, because then he could be invisible. "See me now!" He clapped his hands and Allie gasped.

"Well that's just amazing."

James giggled. Dawn wasn't convinced that he believed he was invisible but he was enjoying himself, so it didn't really matter.

"Allie, did you hear about Wallace?" Laura asked.

"No…" Allie glanced at Dawn and Dawn shook her head.

"He's a she and she had babies."

"Really?" Allie raised her eyebrows. "That's amazing."

Dawn bit her lip to hold her laughter in. She had told her friend about the replacement guinea pig's surprise delivery the previous Tuesday, when she'd met up with her friends at the café, but she'd told Allie that the children would probably want to tell her all about it themselves.

"I had my suspicions that something was wrong because Wallace was so fat." Laura nodded.

"You did?"

"Yes. And… the strangest thing was that his… *her*… eyes changed colour."

"Did they?" Dawn blurted the question before she could stop herself.

"Oh yes. I noticed that there was something different about Wallace at the same time I noticed that she was fatter."

"I see." Rick's smile was getting bigger by the minute.

"Wallace's eyes were pinky-red but they changed to blue.

It must have been because she was going to have babies." Laura folded her arms and turned to Dawn. "When will your eyes change colour, Mummy?"

Dawn gulped under her daughter's scrutiny and Allie snorted loudly.

"What? What's wrong?" Laura asked. "Why is that funny?"

Rick squeezed his daughter's shoulder. "We'll talk about it later, angel. I think Mummy and I need to explain a few things to you."

"Yes, I think we do," Dawn said.

"Oh, okay. Can we go and get a drink, Mummy?" Laura asked.

"Of course."

Laura and James went over to the drinks table and James tugged on Jordan's furry tail. Jordan kept turning around, pretending not to know who was there.

"Well that's something we can't allow her to believe, Rick." Dawn shook her head. "I think we'll have to tell her the truth about Wallace."

"She's pretty sensible, Dawn, so I think she'll understand why you did it." Allie smiled.

"I think she will, too. At least if she is sad about Wallace the first, the new guinea pigs will help to cheer her up. Although I do miss the original Wallace, I have to be honest."

"Well you'll have our new baby to cheer you up soon." Rick slid his arm around Dawn's shoulders. "And this is yet another amazing party, Allie."

"Most of this was down to Jordan and Max. They're a very efficient couple. Although, I have to admit that Chris did prepare a lot of the food."

"Again? Wow, he's definitely a keeper." Dawn didn't try to

hide her delight from Allie. She was so happy that her friend had found such a good man.

"Come and have a look at the food. It's incredible."

"I'll keep an eye on the children." Rick kissed Dawn's cheek.

She went over to the long trestle table that was covered in an orange cloth, and eyed the Halloween delights that Chris had made that afternoon. Savoury foods included witch fingers, ham and cheese bread bones, mummy dogs, pumpkin risotto and cheese and pretzel broomsticks. Then there were toffee apples, chocolate apples, chocolate bat-shaped cookies, meringue ghost tartlets and mini mice cakes.

Chris was standing behind the trestle table wearing a black suit and cape, complete with drawn-on widow's peak and plastic fangs.

"Hello, Dawn! Can I offer you a mummy dog?"

She laughed. "Not just yet thank you, Nosferatu, but they do look delicious."

"Nothing but the best for the village." He winked. "You might also want to try the blood beetroot mocktail that Jordan is serving. The cocktail version is pretty tasty but I know that at the moment..." He nodded at her bump.

"No alcohol for me." Dawn placed a hand on her belly. "Only another twenty or so weeks to go, depending on whether baby comes early, on time or late. And even after she arrives, I'll be unable to drink for a while if I'm breast-feeding."

She realised Allie and Chris were staring at her.

"What? Is it because I said breastfeeding?"

Allie's eyes had filled with tears.

"No. You said... *she*."

Dawn gasped. "So I did! We weren't going to tell people

but we found out at the twenty-week scan. Rick said not to ask but it was quite clear that there was no little penis there."

"Oh that's so wonderful! Congratulations!" Allie hugged her.

"Don't say anything, though. We need to tell Laura and James first and I don't think our son will be too pleased."

"He wants a brother?" Chris asked.

"Really badly. And after finding out that Wallace number two was a girl, well... he feels outnumbered."

"You can always try for a boy next time." Allie winked.

"We'll see. I know we're making some big changes to our lives but this baby was a surprise, so I don't know about a fourth one."

"And sorry about the hiccup with Wallace." Chris shook his head. "It was just such a rush to find a replacement that I didn't think to check. And then for her to be pregnant on top of it."

"Don't worry about it. The children are delighted to have all the pups too."

"Shall we get a drink?" Allie asked.

"Lovely."

At the drinks table, Allie ladled a ruby coloured liquid into two plastic cups.

"Do you want to sit down?"

Dawn nodded so they took seats under the pergola.

"How're you feeling now?" Allie asked.

"Much better. Clearing the air was the best thing we could have done. And now that Rick is going to be home all the time... well..." Dawn leaned back in her seat and stared up at the tiny pumpkin lights. "I just feel so lucky."

"I'm so glad it worked out for you both."

"Thank you for being there for me. You're such a good friend."

"Stop it or you'll have me tearing up again."

"Anyway, cheers!" Dawn held out her plastic cup. "Here's to the future."

"A future that looks very bright indeed."

They tapped their cups together.

"And how is Fenella?"

Dawn had outlined the basics about her chat with her mother-in-law when they'd met up last week, and about their plans for Fenella to visit more regularly, but she'd held back the more personal details, of course.

"Well... I told Rick about how his mother was feeling; I couldn't keep it from him really, and he insisted on speaking to his father. Paul admitted that he'd probably got a bit carried away with his hobbies since he retired, then he promised to make more of an effort with his wife. I rang Fenella yesterday to ask if she's coming to stay this Thursday, and she said she'd have loved to but she can't as Paul is taking her to Cornwall... Poldark spotting!"

"No!" Allie laughed.

"Yes! She's delighted. She even asked me if I thought she might see Aidan with his shirt off."

Allie clutched her stomach as she laughed and Dawn covered her bump with her hands; the baby was fluttering there, as if she was enjoying the joke too.

"I hope you told her to take lots of photos if she does see him."

"Of course."

"Hello darlings!" Camilla sashayed towards them. "What's so funny?"

Dawn's jaw hit the ground as she looked at her sister's outfit.

"Camilla, that's what I call a costume." Allie wolf-whistled. "It's like that scene out of Grease when Sandy turns up all sexy."

"Are you all right, Dawn?" Camilla asked.

"Yes... fine... I just saw your... costume and... wow!"

"It's a little something I had in the cupboard."

"You fibber."

"Okay, well it's a little something I ordered especially for this evening."

"From the cat-alogue?" Allie giggled.

"I don't care where you got it from, Camilla, but I don't think it's appropriate for a children's party." Dawn eyed her sister. "It's barely there."

Camilla was wearing a metallic-black wet-look jumpsuit with a zip-up front, slashed leg detailing and cut out shoulders. It clung to her svelte frame like a second skin. To top it off, she had on a black cat mask that covered her eyes and forehead and sparkled with silver glitter. Her short dark hair had been gelled into spikes.

"I've just popped by to say hello. I'm off to another party later on."

"Oh?" Dawn raised her eyebrows.

"Yes, *oh*." Camilla grinned.

"In the village?"

Camilla nodded.

"Is it at the new vet's house?" Allie asked.

"That's the one."

"We had invites too but I didn't really fancy going. I'm quite partial to my evenings on the sofa followed by an early night." Dawn thought about the past couple of nights, where after the children had gone to bed, she and Rick would cuddle up on the sofa and watch TV together. It was so nice, so much better than sitting alone wondering what time he'd come home. She had asked Rick if he wanted to go to the fancy-dress party, suggested asking her mother to babysit, but he'd told her he just wanted to know his children were safely tucked up in bed and that his wife was in his arms. It was almost like they were rediscovering each other all over again and Dawn knew that she didn't want to be anywhere else of an evening either. There would be plenty of time for parties and the like after baby number three joined them.

"Chris and I would have gone too but it'll be late by the time we've cleaned up here and he's got edits to work on tomorrow, so a late night isn't the best thing for him."

"Well you party poopers, I intend to enjoy myself."

"Hold on..." Allie placed a finger on her lips. "Isn't the new vet... what's his name—"

"Tom." Camilla blurted.

"That's it! Tom Stone. Isn't he pretty good-looking?"

Dawn watched her sister's cheeks darken.

"He's all right. For a vet."

"Is that why you're looking so sexy?" Dawn giggled. "You fancy the vet."

"I do not." Camilla pouted. "And keep your voices down, won't you? I don't want this getting back to him."

"What because that outfit won't give him ideas?"

"You know I don't date anyone from the village," Camilla said. "It's far too risky to get involved with someone local."

"Perhaps he'll offer you a free examination though." Allie snorted. "You know, with you being a cat and all. He might even take your temperature..."

"Oh stop it." Camilla flicked the stick on tail that she'd been toying with. "I'm just going to a party, I'll have a few drinks then I'll head home. *Alone.*"

"Just be careful." Dawn pointed a finger at her sister. "But have fun."

"What's all this then?" Rick asked as he joined them.

"Camilla's having a night on the tiles." Allie blurted.

"She's like a cat on a hot tin roof." Dawn added.

"Watch you don't get stuck in the cat flap if you get home late." Rick joined in.

"Right, that's it, I'm off. I'm not staying here for you to poke fun at me."

"Ring me in the morning." Dawn met her sister's green eyes. "Let me know how it goes."

"Okay, Dawnie." Camilla kissed her cheeks then Allie's before sauntering along the path and out onto the street.

"I hope she knows what she's doing," Allie said.

"She probably does. My sister never does anything without thinking it through. Although he must be pretty special if she's breaking her no dating anyone from the village rule."

"Let's hope so. Anyway, I'd better go and give Chris a hand." Allie got up and took Dawn's empty cup. "You want a refill?"

"Not just yet, thanks."

"Why's Camilla so dressed up?" Rick sat next to Dawn.

"Fancies the vet."

"Does she now? But Camilla never dates anyone local."

"Perhaps this time is different."

"I take it he's hot then?" Laughter danced in his eyes.

"I have no idea."

"You can tell me."

"I haven't seen him yet."

"Shall we fabricate an animal emergency so we can check him out?"

"Rick..." Dawn nudged him. "We can't do that."

"Sure we can. Actually we've had an animal emergency, haven't we? We could ask him to come round to check on the baby guinea pigs."

"Oh, I don't know."

"Don't you want to make sure he's good enough for Camilla?"

"I'm sure she can take care of herself. She's been doing it for long enough."

Camilla had protected her heart for all of her adult life, but Dawn always worried that her sister would get hurt at some point. If she hadn't already been hurt that was. After all, it wouldn't be like Camilla to let on if she had been.

Squeals of excitement broke into her thoughts and she looked over to where Jordan was guiding tiny ghosts, pumpkins, fairies, witches and skeletons around the garden. It seemed that some of the children were looking for clues in some sort of monster treasure hunt. Max, meanwhile, was supervising the games of Frankenstein bowling, which involved knocking down tins painted with monster faces, and every time someone hit them over, there was a loud cheer.

"We're so lucky to live in Heatherlea," Dawn said, as Rick wrapped an arm around her shoulders.

"Wouldn't want to be anywhere else."

"Are you sure?" Dawn asked her husband as she gazed into his eyes.

"Never been more certain about anything. I love you Dawn Dix-Beaumont and I always will do."

He cupped her chin then kissed her gently.

"Oh!" she gasped.

"What is it?"

"Feel." She guided his hand to her belly and he smiled.

"Little one is busy tonight."

"She certainly is."

"Just like her mum always is."

"Not as much now that you're home."

"And I bet she'll be beautiful... just like her mum."

"Thank you."

"No, Dawnie, thank you."

"What for?"

"For making me happier than I could have wished for."

Dawn sighed with contentment as she snuggled into him.

"I'm happier than I ever could have imagined too."

And they stayed that way for some time, on a perfectly cool and crisp autumn evening, watching their two children as they played on the lawn of The Cosy Cottage Café.

Life wasn't always perfect; there were bumps and grooves in the road, and there would no doubt be more ups and downs along the way. But Dawn and Rick had each other and their wonderful family, so they knew that they would be okay.

THE END

ALSO BY THIS AUTHOR…

If you enjoyed *Autumn at The Cosy Cottage Café*, you might also enjoy *Winter at The Cosy Cottage Café*

Chapter 1

"Would you like it wrapped?"

"I'm sorry?"

"The scarf. Is it a gift for someone?" The shop assistant blinked, drawing Camilla's attention to the larger-than-life false black lashes that surrounded her big blue eyes.

"Oh! Yes… yes, please."

Camilla nodded and watched as the younger woman, who could well have been a university student with a Christmas job, produced a perfect square of gold foil paper then wrapped the gift effortlessly, before adorning it with a shiny red bow.

"There! How's that?"

"Fabulous, thank you so much."

"Would you like a bag?"

"No, thanks. I'll tuck in here." Camilla held up her Marc

Jacobs leopard-print cotton-canvas tote – that had cost her over three hundred pounds in July, then she'd spotted in the sales a week later with fifty percent off – and the shop assistant nodded her approval.

Camilla slipped her credit card from her purse and slid it into the payment machine on the counter. As she went through the familiar process of typing in her pin then waiting for the transaction to be processed, she gazed around the department store. Bright strip lights in the ceiling gave everything a surreal glow and bounced off shiny surfaces, mirrors and metallic clothes stands. (She was surprised the shop workers didn't have permanent migraines.) People shuffled around like penguins, weighed down by their shopping bags, picking up items then discarding them as their eyes were drawn to other, better gifts. Strategically placed Christmas trees dressed with this year's must-have festive decorations reminded shoppers that Christmas was on its way and that they didn't have long to find the perfect presents for colleagues, friends and loved ones. And from the speakers around the store, carols blared, adding to the sense of urgency while disguising it as a time of fun, relaxation and togetherness.

Scarf paid for, Camilla tucked her card back into her purse then took the gold package from the counter and carefully put it into her bag. She wished the shop assistant a merry Christmas, but the woman was already peering at the next customer. Camilla sighed; a handsome young man carrying a box of luxury crackers and a pair of corduroy slippers had quickly replaced her.

She pushed her way through the crowds, which wasn't easy as she was going against the flow, then emerged onto the cold street where she gratefully filled her lungs with the icy December air.

Despite her best intentions, she had failed to complete all of her Christmas shopping by mid-November, and instead, it was the first weekend of December and Oxford Street was heaving. Still, there was no time to regret being disorganised; she had gifts to buy, so she'd better get on with it.

She hoisted her tote onto her shoulder then set off towards Selfridges. The regal exterior of the department store always lifted her spirits with its towering stone columns and the ornate clock at the building's main entrance. The window displays were as famous as the store itself, and the Christmas ones always attracted a lot of excitement and attention.

Camilla stopped in front of the nearest window and smiled. It featured a ski lift with Santa Claus in his traditional red suit the middle, with skis strapped to his feet, and on either side of him sat two mannequins. They wore festive outfits and ice-skates as if they were ready to slip off the lift and onto the ice at any moment. Beneath the lift was a pile of soft white snow that looked good enough to dive into headfirst, and tiny white reindeer frolicked at the front of the window.

Camilla moved along and found a space at the next window. This time, Santa Claus was decked out in a red sequin outfit with his fur trimmed hat perched at a jaunty angle on his head. He was emerging from a white personal jet and in each hand he held a lead, at the end of which were two grey toy poodles. In this scene, one of the mannequins wore checked pyjamas while the other wore a knee-length fur gilet and high waisted blue trousers. Suitcases lay scattered around them and some of them were open, spilling their contents – including hot water bottles, fluffy socks and hats – onto the snow. The scene was framed by towering evergreens decked with sparkling white fairy lights. As she gazed at the plane, Camilla wished, not for the first time, that she'd arranged to go away for Christmas. After all, it wasn't as if she hadn't had offers...

Harlan Wright, a long time friend of Camilla's, had invited her to New York for a ten-day trip. A native New Yorker, he jetted around the world with his freelance photography business. The first time Camilla had met him, at a bar in Soho, he'd raved about her looks and told her she could be the modern day Elizabeth Taylor with her delicate features and cropped dark hair. Camilla had been three Manhattans in by then and suspected he was hitting on her until he'd introduced her to his boyfriend, Lance Havisham, a movie extra who'd appeared in lots of films Camilla had never heard of and didn't think she ever wanted to watch.

She'd also been invited to spend Christmas with Malcolm Ferguson, a Scottish Venison farmer. They'd been introduced by a mutual acquaintance at an international rugby match. Malcolm was a giant of a man with a fashionably bald head and thick sandy beard, and had once played rugby himself, but been forced to quit because of a shoulder injury sustained when he was kicked by a pregnant doe. Camilla quite fancied Malcolm, but apart from a physical attraction to him, there wasn't much else she was drawn to and she'd worried that accepting his invitation to snuggle in front of a smouldering yule log while sipping Scotch might send the wrong message.

Then there had been William Roscoe, the wealthy Englishman ten years her senior, who reminded her of Hugh Grant. She had a very soft spot for William. In fact, she had, up until October, wondered what it might be like to allow her friendship with him to develop into something more permanent. Though she hadn't admitted this to anyone else, of course. He had money, a large house in Kent, and a villa in Malcesine on Lake Garda, and he'd asked her to fly to Italy with him and some friends to enjoy Christmas at the lake. But she'd hesitated when he'd invited her, not really sure why at the time, although she'd told him it was because her mother would need her at home to help with the festivities.

In reality, there was another reason why she couldn't bring herself to accept, and Camilla knew it was a very silly reason indeed. It had something to do with a particular vet…

"Penny for them!"

Camilla turned to find her close friend, Allie Jones, smiling at her from beneath a woolly russet beret.

"Allie…" Camilla flung her arms around the other woman's neck, delighted to have been rescued from her thoughts.

"You okay, lovely?" Allie asked as Camilla released her.

"Yes… well, kind of. It's just great to see you. Is Chris with you?" Camilla peered over Allie's shoulder and scanned the crowds for the George Clooney lookalike.

"No, I came into London alone today so I could shop in peace. Jordan and Chris are looking after the café."

"Well if I'd known, I'd have caught the train with you."

Allie smiled. "It was a bit last minute to be honest but now we're here, why don't we go shopping together?"

"That's a great plan." Camilla hooked her arm through Allie's. "And how about if we start with a glass of bubbly in the Selfridges Champagne Bar?"

Allie's blue eyes lit up. "You had me at bubbly!"

"Come on then."

They made their way through the crowds admiring the window displays, and into the department store, with

Camilla nursing a secret delight that she'd bumped into her friend, because Allie would take her mind off her own musings as well as helping her to make the most of the festive atmosphere.

"I don't think I should have had two glasses of champagne, Camilla. You're a bad influence." Allie giggled as they wandered around brightly-lit Wonder Room in Selfridges. "What if I accidentally buy something really expensive?"

Camilla smiled. "You deserve it."

"Not if I bankrupt myself and Chris in the process."

Camilla shook her head. "I'm sure he'd live in a cardboard box as long as it was with you."

Allie blushed and her eyes took on that far away look she got whenever Chris was mentioned. "I'm so happy, Camilla. I still have to pinch myself every morning when I wake up and see his handsome face on the pillow next to me, just to make sure I'm not dreaming."

"You deserve to be happy, Allie. You weren't for a long time."

Allie had spent years single after the death of her husband Roger. She had focused on being a mother to her children and on building her business The Cosy Cottage Café. Her daughter, Mandy, lived in London where she worked in publishing, and her son, Jordan, helped run the café along with his boyfriend, Max. That summer, author Chris Monroe had returned to the village of Heatherlea for his mother's funeral and realised that the feelings he once had for Allie – before her marriage to Roger – were still there. Luckily, the feeling was mutual. They were so in tune that Camilla often thought they could have been together for years not months, as if time had fallen away and they'd never been apart.

"And what about you, Camilla?" Allie squeezed her arm as they stopped in front of a glass display case full of sparkling diamond engagement rings. "Still no one special?"

Camilla suppressed a groan. She loved her friends and her sister, Dawn, but they often asked her about her own love life and it wasn't something she'd ever liked to discuss. Mainly because she felt that if she kept it to herself, then it would remain uneventful and within her control, just the way she liked it.

"Nope. You know me, Allie. I'm independent and that's the way I want to stay."

"Just because you have a relationship with someone, it doesn't mean you have to lose your independence."

"I know. But I do worry that I would. If I ever fell in love." She sighed. "Which is never going to happen."

"Never say never." Allie leaned forwards to look at some of the rings. "Ooh! I almost forgot about the vet. Still nothing going on there?"

Camilla cringed. For the past month, since Halloween in fact, she'd done her best to avoid these questions from Dawn and her friends and had become adept at changing the subject quickly to divert their attention.

"Let's go and look at the Cartier watches. You know they make some of the finest—"

"Oh no you don't!" Allie shook her head. "Not today, Camilla Dix. I know you've avoided this question since the Halloween party at the vet's house… What's his name again? Tom Stone isn't it? Anyway, I want to know what happened and I'm not moving until you tell me."

Allie crossed her arms and stood facing Camilla, her blonde eyebrows meeting above her nose and her mouth screwed into a pout. Camilla couldn't help herself; she burst into laughter.

"What? What's funny?"

"You, you daft woman. Scowling doesn't suit you, Allie. You're far too sweet for that."

"See... distraction techniques again. Just tell me what happened."

"Okay. Okay. I will. But it's not a pretty story."

Camilla took a deep breath and glanced around to check that no one was in danger of accidentally eavesdropping, then she met Allie's curious gaze before exhaling.

"So you really want to know?"

"I do."

"Okay then. On Halloween, I went to the party..."

DEAR READER

Thank you so much for purchasing *Autumn at The Cosy Cottage Café*. I hope you enjoyed reading it as much as I enjoyed writing it.

Did the story make you smile, laugh or even cry? Did you care about the characters? Who do you want to know more about in a future book?

If you can spare five minutes of your time, I would be so grateful if you could leave a short review. Genuine word of mouth helps other readers decide whether to take a trip to The Cosy Cottage Café too.

Wishing you all the best and hoping you'll come back to Heatherlea soon!

You can find me on Twitter @authorRG and at my Facebook page Rachel Griffiths Author.

With love,

Rachel X

ACKNOWLEDGMENTS

Firstly, thanks to my gorgeous family. I love you so much! XXX

Special thanks to Emma LJ Byrne at The Felted Badger for the beautiful cover.

To my author and blogger friends, for your support, advice and encouragement and to everyone who has interacted with me on social media – and supported me – huge heartfelt thanks. This is a crazy, exciting journey and I'm having a great time with you all!

To everyone who buys and reviews this book, thank you. Without you, there would be no Cosy Cottage Café.